S A P

Previously published by John Swan:
the Rouge Murders

To Di
Blue Mountain
July 27/04

SAP
a mystery

John Swan

John Swan

INSOMNIAC PRESS

National Library of Canada Cataloguing in Publication Data

Swan, John, 1949-
    Sap: a mystery / John Swan.

ISBN 1-894663-54-3

I. Title.

PS8587.W343S36 2003   C813'.54   C2003-904819-5

The publisher gratefully acknowledges the support of the Canada Council, the Ontario Arts Council and the Department of Canadian Heritage through the Book Publishing Industry Development Program. We acknowledge the support of the Government of Ontario through the Ontario Media Development Corporation's Ontario Book Initiative.

Printed and bound in Canada

Insomniac Press
192 Spadina Avenue, Suite 403
Toronto, Ontario, Canada, M5T 2C2
www.insomniacpress.com

THE CANADA COUNCIL | LE CONSEIL DES ARTS
FOR THE ARTS | DU CANADA
SINCE 1957 | DEPUIS 1957

ONTARIO ARTS COUNCIL
CONSEIL DES ARTS DE L'ONTARIO

Thanks to Mike O'Connor, Richard Almonte, Adrienne Weiss and Marijke Friesen at Insomniac Press for their many suggestions helping to shape this book. Thanks also to the many who have helped me see the error of my ways, including R.W. Megens, Chris Pannell and Peter Sellers who took the time and trouble to direct me toward the straight and narrow. And finally, to the real Meg Maloney, my love and apologies.

Prologue or Something

Every two-bit dick-yarn starts with a beautiful woman. They stride in on long legs with longer tales of woe and misunderstanding. They've got clear, transluscent skin and hair that rolls in waves over delicate shoulders. Their eyes are liquid pools. Before you can shake their soft hands they have you imagining the shape of their breasts, like Rita Hayworth backlit in *Gilda*, right through a wool plaid shirt. Only Rita wasn't wearing anything like wool, and neither do the rest until you've gotten to know them. Then it's too late.

They've got succulent lips that make grown men talk mush. Chandler said they could make a bishop kick out a stained glass window, and he's the one to know. I'm seldom close enough to threaten church glazing, but it's because of Meg my chevy is parked in some Toronto lot, doors and trunk caved, hole kicked in the front grille, seats and carpeting pulled out, blood all down the rear passenger panel.

Chevrolets may roll off the Oshawa assembly line every two point whatever minutes, but this was my chevy, big and brown. Eight cylinders big. Put a side of beef in the trunk, load the seats with enough rye and beer for a police picnic and it still blew by an eighteen-wheeler and two camper vans one straight shot up the passing lane. Not that that's such a good idea in these zero-tolerance times, not even for an ex-cop barely under the influence. Well I've slept in the chevy, come to that.

Keeping it wasn't easy. It sucked gas like a happy dentist. Lately it'd have meant a missed mortgage payment if it broke down, which thank God and a guy named Larry in a grease-stained jumpsuit, it hardly ever did. I'm past mortgages now anyway, and the chevy was well into a second go round the odometer. I bought it new when Peggy was in grade school. Liz, my wife, was still alive. It carried her to the hospital and home again that last time. It was paid for, it was shit brown, and it counted in miles.

At least, it did until Meg came along.

Part 1

Part I

I

She carries the weighted, black leather sack into the kitchen pinched between her forefinger and right thumb, arm extended. Then left-handed she takes the cigarette from her mouth and, after a quick nod to blow smoke at the ceiling, asks, "What's this?"

Steve, bent to sip from a just filled mug, looks up and blinks. Meg comes as a bit of a shock to him. He rests his coffee on the plastic placemat that marks his parking spot at the breakfast table and pulls his bathrobe to cover the undershirt he's slept in, the fabric near as thin as his chest.

"A sap," I say.

Meg drops it on the maple veneer chipboard between Steve and me. It makes a dull thud. "What for?" she asks.

"To sap people," I say.

She crosses to the counter and starts poking through cupboards.

"You sap saps," Steve says then looks to Meg and me with a loopy grin.

I'm not the type to be critical of folk's troubles—walk a mile in another man's shoes and all that shit—but you'd think his folks could have done something about that mouthful of teeth before sending Steve out to greet the world. "Guys who get sapped must be saps," he spits, "to get sapped. Right?"

Meg looks back over her shoulder. "You should dress when you come down for breakfast. In polite company."

Meg is dressed. She wears the same basic little black sarong she wore last night and must have carefully laid out in my bedroom to keep from wrinkling. She's atop the same heels she strode in on. Not so much as a run in her stockings. Well, I've been a good lad, then.

Same as Steve, I'm wearing a bathrobe. Sleeping raw of late, seeing as it knots the bedclothes less than when I slept fully dressed and relied on Heaven Heather to put me under.

"Hi. I'm Meg Maloney," she says, coming back across the kitchen to Steve, her hand out. "And you must be..." Steve wipes his hands on his robe before taking her soft fingers.

I catch my cue. "Ah, this is Steve Young. Rents the spare bedroom. The one next to mine, where you slept. Steve, this is Meg, my blind date from last night." Steve's lips part enough to reveal a crooked bicuspid. "You can kill that grin. I slept in the sewing room."

The house is a three-bedroom brick pile opposite a park on the Niagara Escarpment that looks out over my city. Liz and I only had the one daughter, fitted the third bedroom up for occasional guests and as an office for me and sewing room for her. I needed an office like I need another asshole. Liz sewed, until she died. I haven't been in the room since, until last night anyway. It needs dusting.

"It's a long story that involves drink and lost keys," I tell Steve. "I'll make up something dirty about it for you later on. For now, all you need to know is Meg's our guest."

I turn to Meg. "Steve is an artist. He's got a commission from the city, haven't you Steve?"

She and Steve shake hands, down and up once.

✦ ✦ ✦

A fancy restaurant in an old mill like the kind Liz had always wanted to go to for anniversaries, except we never got around to it. The smell of fresh bread piped into the dining room, and the sound of a creek trickling outside the window. Here in the pisser, water sounds meant the automatic toilets had flushed.

Neighbours had fixed me up. Blind date, Sue-Anne reaching into her duffel-sized purse, pulling out one of Robbie's old ties and whispering: "Why don't you go to the men's room and slip this on?" Fucking tie already knotted.

I'd thought they were being neighbourly, a night out with their crowd. I'd accepted because of Robbie. The retired pharmacist missed Liz almost as much as I did. They'd been fair-weather friends, meeting in the park across from our house while I tried to snooze before nightshifts. Liz seemed to enjoy their talks. So when he asked me to join this shindig, I brushed lint from my blue blazer and threw down a splash of Heaven Heather to start off in a convivial mood.

"You're going to love Meg," Sue-Anne said, "Besides, you've been rattling around that big old house so long I'm sick of seeing your sad face mooning out the kitchen window."

Should have seen it coming. I slipped the tie into my jacket pocket and grinned at my evil mirror twin. "Think there's a back way out of here without setting off a fire alarm?" He didn't know.

When I returned to the dining room another couple stood at our table. Catching my sleeve, Robbie rose and introduced them. The Crandalls, Veronica and Jim. Jim shook my hand. He was in insurance. How was my coverage? We sat. Seriously, would my dependents be adequately protected if something untimely should happen?

Veronica waved a purple, silk scarf and pecked little kisses at her friends. Not me. Maybe the jury was still out on me after all. Husband Jim took the chair next to Robbie as Stan and Marcie Walters arrived.

"Hello everyone," Marcie said, then sat down quietly.

So quickly we were seven. The waitress came with her pad and pen. I ordered a beer. Veronica told me I would simply love Meg.

Stan was a former high school phys. ed, health sciences and math instructor. Also the wrestling coach and generally a guy who told it like it was. "Kids today need to know how it is. Nobody will tell them anymore."

"So tell me this, Stan. Am I the only one here didn't know I was getting set up with this Meg woman?"

"The girls arranged it. A bit quick off the mark if you ask me. Meg's a real sweetheart, but there's bound to be some pain still, after the shock. She's a sensitive gal, so go slow, okay? Let us get to know you're a right guy. Catch my drift?"

"Shock?" I asked.

"Her husband, Ham. Good guy. Did my taxes for thirty years, no charge. Had to twist his arm to get him to take so much as a bottle in payment, and even then, next time we're at his house, he'd take the lid off and serve it right back at ya."

Stan went thoughtful, pushed his lips in and out staring deeply into his water glass. "Taught me something," he added finally. "Taught me to be more generous with the brand of whiskey I give out, for one thing. Anyway, he's dead now."

"How'd that happen?"

"Water accident up at the cottage. Last summer. Gonna miss him."

"I'm going to miss our cottage weekends." This was Jim, giving Robbie a rest.

"Meg got the cottage in the will. Our guy Swan here gets her out of her funk, we could all be together again, except Ham of course."

"Janet told me she and Ham shared title. That means she gets the cottage, whatever it says in the will."

"Janet?" I asked Sue-Anne across the last empty seat that awaited our guest of honour.

"Ham's first wife."

"So what happened to him? Ham."

Stan again. "I already told you. It was foolish, really, swimming alone that time of night. I mean, Ham was no kind of swimmer. Not much of an athlete at all."

"Then you shouldn't have taken him skinny-dipping," Veronica said.

"For crying out loud, I've said a thousand times, he was just fine when we left him on the dock. It was cold, so we were barely in and out again. But he wanted to stay by the lake, so what were we supposed to do? Knock him down and drag him back to the cottage? I suppose if you'd been there you'd have made him come up to the cottage?"

"Well I don't know what I could have done. I was in bed, wasn't I, long before you decided to throw caution into the lake." Veronica seemed unable to talk without waving her scarf around. "Anyway, the constable said Ham might have been doing anything, and fallen in."

"Like what? What would Ham have been doing down at the lake if not swimming, eh? Feeding the mosquitoes?"

The waitress finally brought drinks and two baskets of buns. Nobody spoke while buttering. My beer was flat.

"There'd been, well, a little much to drink," Marcie said. Sheepish looks around the table. "I'm sure Ham wouldn't have stayed on the dock otherwise. Not alone, that late at night. You just never know what can happen, one slip and no one around to help. Nobody's blaming you Stan." She rested a hand on her husband's sleeve.

"I was out like a light," Veronica said. "Normally I can pace myself and hang in there, not miss a thing. Last to bed, first to rise, but I was so tired that night, and I could hardly drag myself out of bed next morning."

"Must have been the long drive up."

"The Muskoka air."

"Remember you'd been having trouble sleeping around that time. You were probably just worn out," Jim added.

"Look people," Robbie said. "Let's not talk death tonight. That won't change anything. Sue-Anne wanted us together again. If it can't be at the cottage, so be it. Ham is gone. Let's remember the good times we shared."

Jim agreed. "Yes. I for one would like to remember Ham on the hoof, so to speak. His warmth. His generosity."

"Yes." Sue-Anne raised her glass. Dry white wine she'd ordered.

"And his thoughtful consideration for family. Do you know, he called me last year and tripled his life coverage? What finer display of familial love?"

Sue-Anne looked ready to throw her roll at Jim. The waitress coming to take our orders was all that saved him.

Everybody ordered, not waiting for this Meg to arrive.

Marcie turned to me. "Sue-Anne used to say Meg had women's intermission," she said. "She never arrived before anything was half over."

Everything about Marcie was small, the gold chain connecting the corners at the neck of her yellow cardigan sweater, the roses on her cotton dress, her mouth, everything. Even her smile was small and quick.

"That can be annoying," I said.

"Well, you know, we adjusted. Ham was married to Janet, and we all liked her, but people change. When their children left home, Ham dropped Janet like that."

She snapped her fingers. Made me jump. "They were a couple straight away?"

"Yes, now that you mention it, I suppose they were. Soon after, anyway. Why?"

"Do you think Meg and Ham had something going while Ham was still married to Janet?"

"Oh! Oh, I don't know. No, I never thought of that. Ham was well-respected in his community."

Drinks were refreshed. I'd hardly touched my flat suds, which to the waitress meant I didn't need a refill.

"And tripled his life insurance for his new wife," I said. "That was thoughtful."

"Well now that's Jim. He's always getting everyone to buy more insurance. He got Ham to take out a new policy because Meg was so much younger, she'd need more money to last after he was gone."

Marcie turned away from me. It would be rude to ignore her friends, though they mostly ignored her. She seemed the only decent one in the lot. Sue-Anne and Robbie had thrown me in with a high-school bully, a scarf-waving fashion diva and a fully pressurized insurance salesman. The beer was flat and I wanted to go home. So naturally, that's when Meg showed up.

✦ ✦ ✦

"What's she do?" Steve whispers when Meg goes back to the cupboards. Steve's tone implies he doesn't believe such a healthy specimen would follow me home. I'm amazed myself. Every strand on her blond head is in place, but not hairspray rigid. It bounces down her back as if guided by some invisible force field invented by Q in the James Bond movies. There's a lot of it too, enough to fill out a rack full of glamour magazine covers.

"Scares shit out of the neighbours," is the first thing comes to my mind. "Keeps husbands too. For a while, at least. Maybe gets rid of them for the proceeds," I continue. Then I raise my voice for Meg. "We didn't get silly last night, did we, fly to Vegas and tie the knot? Mugs are in the cupboard on your right, since you're looking."

"You're safe for now." She pokes through my cupboards like she's sizing up my estate, finally selecting a proper cup. "Only got as far as the blood test." Turns and gives us the benefit of those big, liquid orbs, which are only a little redder and a little more liquid than I remember them last night. She flashes the pearlies again. "That's when you passed out."

I didn't, but I have a reputation with Steve to maintain so I let the accusation stand. Meg flicks ash down the sink and pours coffee. She opens the fridge and finds a carton of milk, pinches out the spout and sniffs. Milk goes in. I swirl the mud at the bottom of my mug and decide to go for the heel still in the pot. She takes my chair soon as I'm up.

"Tell me about this commission you've got," she says to Steve.

"City has a birthday comin'," he says.

I turn to look at him, but that's all there is.

"Big anniversary year. Hundred and twenty-fifth, or hundred fifty. Something like that," I say.

"Let him tell it."

Steve looks surprised. "Yeah, well, like Mr. Swan says. They got money for the arts. Commemorate, celebrate, you know. I'm thinking about a proposal."

Several sentences, some with big words. Steve maybe warming to Meg now there's the possibility she could do me in.

"Thinking? You seemed more definite when you asked me to carry your rent for a couple months," I say from the counter.

Meg looks at me and blows smoke. "Ashtray?" she asks.

I consider going through the backs of cupboards, but find the lid from a jam jar first. "Trade you."

"Didn't think you smoked," she says.

"I'm near fifty," I answer. "The fuck am I saving it for?"

She goes to her purse, opens her pack and puts a Bic on the table. I take one, light up and cough.

Meg freshens, lighting from the dwindling butt she brought downstairs. "I could smoke for the two of us, if you like. Second hand is cheaper, and sexier if you ask me. You ever hit anyone with this sap?" she asks.

Steve watches the conversation like it's a tennis match.

"Now and then," I say. "Carried it on the beat. It was good in a brawl. Sorted things quick."

"Ever hit anyone to get a confession?" She's smiling.

"Maybe whack the table top a few times. Usually does the trick." I take a drag and concentrate on not coughing again. "Saps weren't regulation, but most cops carried one when I was on the force. Safer than a gun. Draw a gun only when you intend to use it, according to regs, and don't get fancy either. That's how bystanders get hurt. Always aim where you're most likely to hit. The torso, where the most damage is done." Meg isn't drinking her coffee. "So you bring out a sap, doesn't automatically mean somebody has to die. Snap a collarbone, crack a kneecap. Puts an end to a lot of shit."

I see it in her eyes. She's going for it.

Until Steve chimes in, "I thought that's what the sticks were for."

I smile. "Saps are backup. Anyway, when you're dicking it, plainclothes, the billies kind of stick out."

"Now the sap sits in your top dresser drawer," Meg says.

"I'm not a cop anymore."

"Still have a gun?"

"Nope." I stub the cigarette, over an inch from the filter.

"Shouldn't you carry something? Just in case? I thought you went private." Meg takes the pack and lights another. She keeps the cigarettes on her side of the table.

I pull the flaps of my bathrobe together, retie the fabric belt. "Not my job to make people behave anymore. I poke around other people's affairs now and then. Not carrying a weapon means I think before making trouble."

"Sounds dull if you ask me. Besides, you didn't throw it away. You still keep the sap at the back of your dresser drawer."

"So?"

"So what is it, a souvenir of happier times?"

Steve's eyes come back to me. "What were you doing in my dresser anyways?" I say.

"Looking for condoms."

Jesus.

Steve gets up to leave.

"You haven't got any bacon or eggs by the way, or anything that might be called breakfast so far as I can see."

"Got coffee haven't you? Should be a carton of juice somewhere. Did you look in the back of the fridge?" I'm thinking I'd like another cigarette, but Meg doesn't offer and maybe I shouldn't ask. She hasn't lifted her cup since carrying it to the table either. "I suppose there's something wrong with the coffee too," I say.

"No, the coffee's just fine."

Silence again.

"No sugar," she says finally.

"Well, I like it black. And that's Steve's milk you just helped yourself to, by the way. And him still a growing boy."

She blows more smoke, not bothering to direct it away from my face. "So how do you use it?" She picks up the sap, the narrow end in her palm, thumb along the shank.

"Break your thumb that way. Tuck it in. Otherwise, that's all there is to it. Watch where you swing."

"It's rather phallic, don't you think?"

"Beg your pardon?"

"Very macho," she says, stroking the leather sack with a red-nailed finger. "Like a scrotum. I see a room full of big men, sitting with their legs open, scratching their Blackjacks. That's another name for a sap, isn't it? Blackjack? Is that what you do at the police-men's ball, haul them out for comparison? Do they come in different sizes? Are there competitions?"

"Okay, put it away."

"Where would you carry it? Can't be in your pocket. It would show in the drape of your suit."

I reach to take it from her hand. "Hooked on the belt, usually. Here, give it to me."

"At the small of the back, I imagine, hanging down the crack..."

"Just give it me." I grab the sap from her hand. She sets back, pouting. Jesus.

"I was only teasing," she says.

II

"When do you get this job from the city?" I ask Steve.

"Soon I guess. I don't know for sure."

"You told me you already had it. How do you expect to pay your rent?"

Steve butters toast, reloading as we chew. I've found bread. And butter. And half a box of Sugar Crisps. I've made a mental note to buy condoms next time I'm out.

"I think what John means is, is there a problem?" Meg asks. "You can tell us if there is."

I give my head a shake. Us? I'm strategizing to get laid and she's already waxing domestic.

"No problem, not really," Steve says. "I got– I've got my proposal in," and then he mumbles something artsy-craftsy. "I can't understand why they don't answer me."

"Who? Who doesn't answer?" Meg asks.

"The guys who give out the money for the anniversary arts projects. The city and some companies put up the money that these two guys are supposed to assign to projects. The notification date for selections passed weeks ago. I phone and there's an answer machine, but they never call back. I go down to the office they have in Jackson Square and there's never anybody there." Steve hesitates. "No. Once, there was a woman. She said leave my name and they'd call me. But they didn't, unless they called and you didn't tell me." This last bit is for me.

"If there was a call for you, Steve, I'd tell you."

"Even if you didn't know who it was? Maybe they didn't say."

"Okay Steve, who are these guys?"

"One I remember—Mike Zabignolski—and the other is a lawyer I think, Geary or O'Leary or something."

"Oh Christ."

"What?"

"Liam O'Leary. Big and Leery. Party bag men in the east end. You're telling me my rent money hangs on some scam they've hatched to carry them over till the next election? Kiss that goodbye." Which I do, fingers to lips in a worldly gesture for Meg's sake. It doesn't seem to take, so I give Steve the hard stare. "You paid first and last when you moved in. Have you got anything for next month, or is this your last?"

Steve peeks from beneath lowered brows.

"So he's not behind yet, I take it," Meg says.

"Come on Steve. Have you got any prospects or do I put a "for rent" in the paper?"

"You can't ask him that. He doesn't owe you anything."

"Not yet," I answer Meg over my shoulder.

"Then quit pestering him. It's none of your business until the rent's due, and then it's none of your business where he gets it," green eyes flashing. Last night I'd taken them for blue.

"Look," I say, "I'm just trying to figure it out. It would be good to know where we're at. He's supposed to give me notice if he's moving out."

"Suppose he's not planning to move out? You're not planning to move, are you Steve?"

Steve says nothing. He's like a rat when the lights come on, eyes scanning for a place to scurry.

"Christ, what am I, the evil landlord? Wait here, will you, while I rush upstairs to wax my moustaches and get some rope to tie you to the railway tracks." I cover half the last slice of toast with butter that won't melt. "Big and Leery. Shit."

Meg's footsteps stomp up the stairs, as loudly as a pair of high-heeled size sevens can stomp. The tone is definitely different than this morning, when she first came down. I get the message. Steve hunkers down over his empty plate, unsure whether to run or stay.

"This family life shit cramps the savoir faire," I tell him. "Let it be a lesson to you."

✦ ✦ ✦

The real deal arrived at last, an hour late for dinner and thirty years late in my life. It was easy to see why Sue-Anne and her lady friends had been eager to play matchmaker. They needed to get this husband-snatcher paired off quick. That they'd chosen me was a measure of their desperation.

Meg gave each couple their own personal greeting: a sisterly kiss for wifey while a hand lingered on hubby's shoulder. Or maybe a little higher, a painted fingernail creeping up behind an ear. I couldn't wait for my turn.

"And you must be John Swan," her hand a soft, white fish. "I've heard so much about you."

"I have no insurance," I told her, taking up the five delicate fingers.

"Not to worry," she said. "I've recently collected plenty thanks to Jim." Not even a blush.

Jim coughed into his napkin. I rolled up my tongue, tucked it back in my mouth, stood and pulled the chair out for her.

"Robbie says you were a police detective. Tell me, does that make you suspicious by nature?"

"Once upon a time. I'm retired now."

It was like no one had ever smiled at me before. "I understand, but that's not really the question, is it? The question is, are you going to investigate me?" She was making her friends uncomfortable. I liked that. "Or have you already started, before we've been properly introduced?"

I had to get my eyes out of her cleavage. She wore what I'd once heard Liz describe as a little black dress. On Meg, it just looked little. Men at other tables snuck glances hoping their wives wouldn't notice.

"Investigate? You? What for?"

"Oh, whatever occupies the minds of policemen who retire early and need something to do with their hands."

I offered her a menu, ran my finger down the page. "I recommend the fresh quail, cooked to the third degree."

Stan was rolling some idea around in his mind. We locked eyes. "Try not to be vulgar," he hissed. "That's hardly what Meg needs right now."

"It's a joke Stan." I turned back to Meg. "No need to feel threatened."

"Threatened?" He slammed down his menu. "Let me tell you something. I was Commonwealth light-heavy wrestling champion three years running. You don't threaten me. I do the threatening, understand? And I can talk circles around you too, come to that."

Stares all round.

"What's the matter, Stan?" Marcie asked.

"Nothing. Nothing's the matter. I just don't like this smartass and his talk about investigations." He pulled on his drink. "We're Meg's friends. We're supposed to be helping her through a difficult time. Not pawn her off on the first...on the first...well look at him!"

"Sorry Stan," I said. "It was a joke. Any real investigation's already been done, by the Provies. They're good as any. Not to mention the insurance company, eh Jim?"

"Of course," Jim said, thankful. "Very thorough. I moved things along as best I could, but they wouldn't have paid out if there'd been any possibility Ham's death wasn't an accident."

"So no one can seriously suspect Meg of doing anything wrong." Faces ducked back behind menus. Meg looked confidently 'round the table.

"Well, I was in bed, asleep," Veronica said.

"Aha! So you say"—Jim making like the manor sleuth, instead of Veronica's insurance-salesman husband—"but did anybody actually see you after you went upstairs?"

"How would I know? I was asleep, wasn't I? Since we're asking, where the hell were you?"

"I was in the kitchen. With Marcie. Playing gin."

"Of course you were. I saw you, just like we all saw Veronica go up to bed," Sue-Anne explained. "The cottage is open, all one big room, except the bedrooms and bathroom of course. Jim and Marcie were at the table, playing cards. I found a good book and curled up on the sofa. Robbie was at the window, straining his eyes."

I smiled at Robbie.

"I had a nightcap to warm up. Then I left Sue-Anne to her book and went to bed by myself," Robbie said.

"So everybody but Ham and Meg were in the cottage? Who alibis Meg?"

"I will," Stan said. "I mean I did. We went for a swim, it was cold so we came back up." Stan looked at Meg. "Meg tried to get Ham to come back with us, said something to him."

"What?"

He shrugged. Meg answered: "I told him to hurry back to the cottage. It was time for bed."

We locked eyes. Hers were blue, complementing her tumble of blond curls. She knew that every male within hearing was thinking that if she told them it was time for bed, they'd have run across that lake to rest their head on her pillow.

I smiled. "And I believe you, just like the Muskoka coppers and the insurance company before me. Of course I do."

The waitress arrived with our food. Meg ordered dinner. Jim caught the waitress's sleeve. "I'll have another scotch-rocks if you don't mind."

"Me too," I said. "Neat." Scotch was made to be served flat.

They tucked in, except Meg, who watched while I ate. I don't remember what it was. Meg said we would become friends. "What do you think we'll have in common?"

I rested my fork, told her I liked baseball and jazz.

"Very predictable," she said. She told me she'd been on her own most of her life, that she was living with an aunt who ran some sort of business out of her home. Meg helped her aunt now and again. She didn't say doing what.

Janet had got the house in the divorce. Ham had got the cottage. He and Meg rented an apartment in town. She wasn't sure what she'd do with the Muskoka cottage yet. Did I like movies?

"You're leaving something out," I told her. She looked puzzled. "You like to tease men."

She smiled and licked the end of her swizzle stick. "I do, yes. Now how about you?"

"Oh I never tease men."

She frowned. "Too corny. Don't try so hard." Her lips were a full and rich red.

My scotch arrived, with soda. I tried to figure where I'd gone wrong with the staff in this place.

Turned out that the Walters and Crandalls had to run before dessert, but Meg and the Robinsons stayed for coffee and drinks.

"*Digestifs*," Sue-Anne called them. I played it safe by ordering coffee. How badly could that be screwed up? I ordered it black, then leaned back and picked some gristle from my teeth. Meg excused herself to go powder her nose. Her words, I swear. I stood to pull out her chair.

She held my eyes with her own. I went for it, pulled her to me and pressed my lips slow and hard to her mouth. People didn't do that in this restaurant. Not the way we did it. When she kissed back I wanted her more. My heart pounded so hard that I thought she must feel it. What did she want from me, I wondered, a tired, fat, middle-aged ex-cop?

We broke. Then she headed for the ladies'.

"You were right," I said to Sue-Anne. "She's hot." I was a kid again.

"You might have shown some consideration," Sue-Anne said.

"Consideration?"

"Ham's death has been very trying for all of us. We were his friends. You might have shown some compassion."

"I don't get to church much, but as I recall compassion follows confession."

"Really? What have I to confess?" Sue-Anne sipped from a small, stemmed glass of crème de menthe. Robbie was drinking tea.

"Did anyone see Stan and Meg come back from the lake?" I asked Robbie. "And did anyone ask you for something to help a body sleep?"

He shot a quick glance at Sue-Anne before shaking his head. "They'd asked about dosages for over-the-counter medication. I'd never supply anything stronger without a prescription. I could. I still know some people. But I wouldn't. Never." Quietly, twisting the napkin in his lap. "There wasn't anything in Ham's bloodstream. The police did an autopsy. A high alcohol count, nothing more."

"No," I said. "Whatever you recommended, it wasn't for Ham. The beauty of it was everyone just had to be themselves. Jim to provide extra insurance. Stan to be protectively possessive. You to provide the pharmacological advice. Everyone to drink, act silly until they passed out. Only Ronnie needed to have her behaviour changed. Your stuff put her to sleep when she would normally have been awake. Once everyone went to bed, someone could take Ham on his last swim."

Sue-Anne had lost her smile. She wore a red silk blouse that covered her arms, and a large Campbell-plaid scarf done up like an inverted kerchief to her neck, anchored by an insect broach.

"I was asleep on the sofa. Somebody moving through the room woke me up. It was dark, the lights were out, but I saw who it was." She sipped her green liquid. "Oh this is fun. I can see why you enjoy it so much, John, but maybe not so much now you've been taken by Meg?"

"Really, Sue-Anne." Robbie didn't like any of it.

"Well, I did fall asleep, but it was fitful. That's what I remember: waking to see Stan; then waking again to see Meg, though I couldn't say how much later. It might have been seconds. It might have been hours."

"Between waking and sleeping, you could have missed anyone come and go entirely," Robbie said. "You could have got the order wrong."

"No," she smiled. "I remember the order. Stan, then Meg."

Robbie: "Then why didn't you tell the police?"

Sue-Anne smiled and shrugged. "Who says I didn't?"

"I was going to ask if you needed a lift." Meg had come up without our noticing. She had her coat.

"I do," I said. "Yes, please."

She handed me the keys. "Do you seriously think I'm capable of murder?" she asked.

"We've only just met. I'm trying to learn not to be judgmental."

"Meaning?"

"You don't know anything about the things I've done," I said.

That explains, more or less, how I found Meg in my kitchen the next morning.

✦ ✦ ✦

I'm stacking dishes in the sink, my back to the table, when Meg's footsteps come back down and onto the linoleum. A smack on the table. "Here."

I turn. A C-note under her palm. "What's that?"

"Steve's next month's rent. Enough?"

"Well, two hundred actually, but..." She goes into her purse, smack, another C-note on the table. "You don't have to..."

"Two hundred a month. There." Her eyes are blue again. Can't be the light.

"You don't have to do that. It's not up to you."

"Consider me a goddamn patron of the arts. What do you care? Just let me know when he's short, for as long as he wants, though why he should choose to live here with you is beyond knowing."

I probably blink first. We turn toward Steve at the same time.

"Oh yes," he smiles. "I like it here fine."

I offer back the two bills. "You don't need to do this. I'm not gonna toss him. Just teaching him some responsibility. I'll go down and see what's what with this art program."

"What'll that accomplish?" she asks.

I snort. "Believe me, I know Big and Leery. When it comes to art, they don't know enough to paint walls. But give them a compelling reason, they'll do what they're supposed to do in the first place."

Meg's lighting up again. "What do you call a compelling reason?"

I have this smile sometimes works on waitresses and stressed checkout girls. It implies empathy though Liz always called it a smirk. "Don't put the sap away, okay?"

"That's it? That's the best you've got?"

"If you ask politely, Big and Leery don't respect you."

Meg clocks the dial over the kitchen window. "When do you plan to do this?"

"There's a rush?"

She looks at the clock again. "I should get going. My Auntie has one of her things this afternoon. I have to be there." She hesitates, considers. "How do you feel about cocktails and weenies on a stick?" Before I can answer, she adds, "About five. I'll introduce you to Auntie and some of my people."

"Anything like Sue-Anne and that crowd?"

"Indulge me. Learn how I actually scrape by. You can keep this." She pushes the two C-notes back in my direction, fingers touching mine under the bills.

"No need. Really. What for?"

"To put a hold on that room down the hall, the one where you slept last night." She sits down and sips from her coffee. "My arrangement with Auntie is temporary, until I find something better. It is available, isn't it, the room?"

I sit. She shifts slightly, brings her thigh next to mine. I pull the two hundred my way.

"Good," she says. "I haven't had a fight like this since Ham kicked."

"My usual policy with new tenants," I tell Meg, "is first and last in advance."

III

I'm not sure how I get to Toronto, Meg on my arm and Toby under-foot. Mostly I take Meg's word for it. What I do remember is the night starts at her aunt's house.

I usually take the corners at these so-called business-is-pleasure affairs. Attended a few when my shyster brother Artie was ass-kissing his way up the legal ladder. Heaven Heather or any decent scotch never make the wine list. Someplace out of the way, the closer to the cloakroom the better, works for downing rye and sodas while arms tire of backslapping. That's why I prefer house parties to banquet halls. More corners, for starters, and coats get stacked in a quiet, remote bedroom. Folks are usually considerate enough to turn out the light after they've chucked theirs onto the pile. Surprising, too, what spills out of pockets at these things.

The downside with house parties is parking. Walking back from the first available spot, there are signs Meg's shindig could be a whole other level of soiree than I've experienced before. For starters, turns out there's valet parking. A young kid in a red vest runs past while I'm resting outside a set of iron gates with a French château behind. Just a mini-château, understand. Not the real thing. The same kid nearly runs me over with a BMW when I finally turn up the curved drive to Meg's aunt's pile. It's a rambly kind of place, nearly hidden behind a couple of low hills sprouting shrubs the way warts sprout hairs on a witch's nose.

A guy at the front door asks to see my invitation. I'm a special guest of Meg's, I tell him. He gives my blazer and slacks the once-over and asks me to wait while he checks. You'd think I hadn't dabbed the soup stains from my tie before heading over. But he doesn't ask "Meg who?" so I know she hasn't been blowing steam about that. Whatever this bun-fest's about, she's among those that cooked it up. I give the security guy about five seconds head start, then make my own way inside.

The hit-and-miss security routine extends into the house. Three different single malts behind the bar and nothing to protect them but a Chinese kid in a red vest and black bow tie. Pouring me a second, he says I'm supposed to sip single malt. His stuff has a fancier label than Heaven Heather, so I promise to give his suggestion a try.

The joint is big enough to have plenty of good hidey-holes, but out of nowhere Meg has her arm through mine. She's steering. Don't know what that perfume is she's wearing, but it smells even better than the scotch. The kid in the vest and bow tie seems relieved to see me go.

"I could give your aunt some tips on security," I say.

"Later. There are people you should meet first," Meg says.

It's Doctor this and Chairwoman that. She's on the board of Whatever and he's a director of Municipal Thingamabobs. There's lawyers I've never seen in a courtroom. None have names I can remember from any of Artie's suck-ups either. Seems the titles on the guest list get more inflated with the quality of the scotch. Pity Artie never learned that.

Or maybe I've been out of action long enough that a new crush of appetites have moved up the food chain. One thing: they don't go formal for these things anymore. Pastel shirts, sweaters hung around necks, jeans with creases pressed into them. The help is better dressed.

"What is the occasion?" I ask a girl that offers me a tray of biscuits topped by bits of pink flesh, red sauce, a sliver of something green. Not a real cocktail weenie in sight. "Somebody's birthday?" I latch on to the edge of the tray.

"I know you're acting like this to impress me with the fact that you're not impressed by my guests," Meg says, pulling me from the hors d'oeuvres tray with one hand while sliding a wafer between my lips with the other. "I want you to know that I'm not impressed by the fact that you're not impressed."

"For one thing—" I've no idea what she's put in my mouth; something crunchy, prickly, "I don't know anybody here so I can't be impressed by them. And for another, you said this was your auntie's party, not yours."

"This is a fundraiser for the Minister of Culture and Heritage. She's going to be Prime Minister some day soon."

"No shit? She here?"

"She has a very busy schedule."

"Then these are the not-yet-ready-for-direct-access supporters?"

"No. These are more your garden variety it-would-be-unseemly-to-be-seen-handing-over-bags-full-of-cash type of supporters."

"Wait now." I press palm to brow. "Am I standing in a smoke-filled back room?"

"An antechamber," she says, producing a napkin to swipe goop from the corners of my mouth. "We do, however, boast an amusing selection of yes-men and gofers, for the discerning political aficionado."

"*C'est moi,*" I say, remembering I've been to high school too.

She leads me to an adjoining room and down two steps to a pit of pink carpet. A fireplace burns gas behind a glass screen. Two wide bums impress a pair of facing, pink loveseats. Big and Leery have drinks in their left hands, their rights free to scarf bickies from the tray they've managed to separate from a passing red vest. Their elbows are up.

"John, I'd like you to meet Mike Zabignolski and Liam O'Leary," Meg says.

They're a coordinated fashion statement. Leery is wearing a dark blue blazer over light blue, checked pants. Big has dark blue slacks and a blazer that matches Leery's pants. They both wear wide blue ties. Ten years ago, last time I saw them give or take, they'd completed this ensemble with matching white belts and loafers. Leery has something in his teeth that gives me hope there's still new and interesting selections to be scooped from a passing food tray.

"Swanee," Big says.

Meg pretends surprise. "You know each other?"

"Big and Leery," I tell her, "used to carry the bag for Sherman police station before it was closed and its crimes hopefully forgotten. Always wondered what happens to guys like you when the revenue stream gets bunged up."

"We moved upstream Swanee," Big answers. He's showing lots of bridgework, but that's probably for Meg's benefit. "You might have done the same. What are you up to lately?"

I feign interest in a faux woodpile beside the fireplace. "Looking for the body of the waiter you mugged for those canapés."

"Mike and Liam manage the City of Art Festival," Meg says.

"No shit. Lame, what do you know about art?"

"It's a new initiative, necessitated by the provincial government's unprecedented and unwarranted withdrawal of funding from local arts programs," O'Leary says. "The Minister and the city have turned to the generosity of the private sector to underwrite the costs of mounting exhibits and performances recommended by the creative community." O'Leary's gotten good enough at the schmooze to run for office himself.

"And you guys know the Minister? Wow. She's some doer eh? To think that only thirty years ago I busted her for drinking under age." Meg's eyes don't flicker.

Big smiles. "I doubt there's a record of that."

"No," I admit. "You're right. Her old man was still mayor then."

"Good old Swanee," Big adds. "You always did know how to impress your betters."

Trying to set me on course, Meg says: "City of Art is the program I think, where Steve has his application."

"We've been charged with collecting donations from the corporate community," O'Leary says. He and Big have the grins of confident men. "And it's Liam, not Lame."

"Congratulations," I say. "You've really fallen into it then. Should tide you over until someone calls another election. Any chance there'll be something left for the artists?"

I'm trying. I really am.

Meg leaves us. My eyes follow her steps back up to the milling sheep. She has a way with walking. That afternoon she'd found time to put her hair up and change from the little black dress to a little red dress.

"Forget it," Big says. "You can skate on that pond, but you'll never sink a line."

I turn back to him. My glass still holds a swallow. "Spent last night at my place," I say, gesturing toward Meg. That gets their attention. "She's talking about moving in." It will break their hearts if I tell them she's paying rent for the privilege, but I show mercy. Besides, mention money, they'd start figuring some way to get a commission.

"Who's this Steve character?" O'Leary asks.

"Kid living at my place till he's back on his feet. Apparently that involves getting his work in your show," I say. "How's it going anyway? Room for one more?"

"Well now," says Big. "We have a very intriguing submission from the Belloni girl. You might remember her father was captain of the old Junior Wings before catching on in Detroit. Has a chain of tire stores now, based out in Burlington, but he still likes to support the old hometown community."

"Her paintings truly capture the urban experience," O'Leary says. "My modest opinion."

"We've also got some wonderful theatre." Big again.

"Showstopper stuff. Peltier Distillery has provided us with a list of suppliers eager to put their names behind *Broadway Bound*. It'll be young Danny Peltier's local, professional debut. He spent six years in New York you know."

"Driving cab?" I ask.

"Probably fucking the junior class at some big-name dance school," Big smiles.

"Don't knock it," O'Leary finishes. "He auditioned for off-off-Broadway chorus lines."

"Stop the presses," I say.

"And don't forget the Fluke Family Drum and Whistle Band." Big again.

"A community favourite." O'Leary.

"Sixty uniformed drummers tooting whistles in intricate rhythm as they perform precision marching maneuvers." Big.

"Right down the centre of King Street." O'Leary.

"You mean like a fife and drum band?" I ask.

"No, no. Sports whistles. With a pea inside?" Big.

"Christ. Who'd pay to see that?" I ask.

"I believe the Flukes are in waste disposal." O'Leary again. "Just won the contract to run the city's sewage plant."

"But I don't think that's what Swanee meant." Big.

"No?"

"No. I think he's wondering who'd put up twenty large to see something slapped together by his tenant."

"Who you recommend, Swannee? Can you suggest a sponsor?"

I skip the Chinese kid's advice and finish my single malt in a gulp.

"No? Well, we'll see what we can do," Big and O'Leary say, turning their backs.

"Needa go," I tell the boys, holding up my empty glass.

"Say," Big says, turning back with the empty canapé tray, "see if you can get this refilled, will ya?"

✦ ✦ ✦

I don't see Meg on my way back to the bar in the family room. Or is it the recreation room, or maybe the rumpus room? I could ask Meg's aunt which is which but we haven't been introduced. When we are, I'll suggest she put up signs. Discreetly, of course.

I throw back the first shot the Chinese kid gives me, and ask him for another and a beer. I figure to get a bottle, but he pulls a glass from a tap mounted on top of a small cooler.

"Hold up on that," I say as he nears the top. I drop the second shot into the glass.

"You come to these things often?" he asks, wiping my splash from his counter.

"I could develop a taste for them. You?"

I wander two more rooms then hover around a foursome talking house pets.

"We had a mutt from the pound," I offer. "Unpredictable on the carpet, but no inbred behaviour or health problems."

Four eyes stare into the dregs swirling round their cocktail glasses. One set scours the room for intelligent life. One set turns my way. "Yes, pound puppies can be quite bright I understand."

"Dog did our income tax for ten years."

Hesitation, then a toothsome grin. "Really, that is smart," she says.

"I dunno. Most years I thought we overpaid." Now all the hooded eyes come to me. "Refill, anyone?"

"Don't you think you've had enough already?"

"Not anymore."

But I find Meg before I find the bar. She's huddled with a group of men in sport jackets, which I guess makes them young sports. One even has a turtleneck under his shirt. Probably a dickie. Haven't seen one of those since high school. *Has his dickie around his neck*, we used to say until Trudeau came along and it changed to *has his ascot around his neck*. I make a mental note to remember the phrase in case there's conversation needs sparkling up.

The circle laughs at something Meg has said. I'm to one side, smiling, waiting for her to notice so I can tell her it's time to go, or at least let me in on the joke.

"Anyone remember when Trudeau was PM and had his ascot around his neck?" someone says using my voice. "Get it? Ass caught around his neck?"

They don't. My glass is empty, but I don't expect to find the bar ever again. The look Meg is shooting, I'm not sure the Chinese kid will oblige if I do. It's already like the waiters carrying around trays full of domestic champagne have been warned to dodge me.

Just beyond the kitchen is a long hallway no one seems to be using. A couple of doors before it hangs a left into what I guess are homey nether regions. Door on the left is a two-piece toilet. Sorry. Joint like this, must be the Powder Room.

Doorway number two leads to, hey, an indoor pool. No one in it. I've time to kill. I could probably use freshening up. I strip to my boxers.

The close end of the room is all concrete block painted blue, the far end is glass on three sides. Doing a combo of breaststroke and dog paddle, I keep my head above water. There's a courtyard full of shrubs and patio furniture. There's Meg beyond the courtyard, through double patio doors, amusing her sports. A sleek arm takes hers. Silver hair, and when he turns slightly toward the window, an ascot is around his neck. They ease out of the room. Several laps, nobody beyond the courtyard notices me. I return the compliment.

"Very graceful." A woman dressed in white, shoes to cap, sitting by the round, glass topped table I passed on my way in. She's chosen the deck chair furthest from the one covered in my currently unemployed clothing.

"Wait'll you see my sidestroke," I say.

"Don't believe I can," she answers, indicating the freshly lit cigarette in her hand. Looks like she's stealing a break from the kitchen. "Vat's your excuse?"

"Olympic trials next week. Meg promised I could use her pool for practice," I say, edging closer to her along the side of the pool, "if I don't scare her guests."

"And who're you that Meg vants you here so badly?"

"Janet Gretzky. I'm surprised you didn't recognize me."

"Vat's your event Janet? Bottom crawl?" She doesn't move to take my extended hand.

"The real Janet would be offended to hear you say that. She's a lovely woman, graceful in a swimsuit like me. I used to dream about her, bouncing on a diving board." I push off from the side.

"You or her?" She has me. "Bouncing on the board, you or her?"

Floating on my back. "Oh. I was in bed, or somewhere dreaming of Janet bouncing on the diving board. She's in an old movie, *Flamingo Kid*. Well before she wed that puck pusher."

Her face is a cloud of smoke. "You're very cultured, in the vay of lonely peckers vith bedroom film fantasies, but still you digress. Vat's your event?"

"Single synchronized," I say and dip my head into an underwater back turn.

"Never understood that," she's saying as I come back to surface. "If it's a single, vat's it synchronized vith?"

"You got me again."

She puts the cigarette to her mouth, takes it out, blows an extended stream of blue smoke out over the water. "Not sure I vant you. I just needed the sit down. These dogs are really barking." Doughy face lined by years of nicotine.

"Take your shoes off, paddle those puppies in the pool. Better yet, first get us a couple glasses of that single malt they've got. Shame to waste all this water without something to splash it in."

She puts her cigarette down, lit end over the edge of the table, holds up one finger and disappears out the door. She's back inside a minute with most of a bottle of Heaven Heather. "Always keep one stashed in the kitchen," she says. "Emergencies."

"I'm in love."

"Me or the bottle?"

Her nose has been broken and her stomach bulges between her D cups and her XL cotton panties, but she has a few moves. She's showing me one, feet waving in the air while she spins up-side-down in the water, when Meg comes to gather me up. The light is dimming in the courtyard.

"Party over?" I ask. "Suitcase packed? Ready to move into my place?"

"Let's put that on hold for tonight." Meg already has the scene sized up.

"You want your two hundred back? Look, see her nails?" I point to my pool pal. "What would you call that colour, sort of metallic green? Ever seen it before?"

"Yes, I've seen it before."

The kitchen help bobs upright and swims to the edge of the pool, where a full tumbler of Heaven Heather awaits. She drains half. The bottle is empty on the table by my elbow. I tell Meg I'd make introductions, but I haven't properly been introduced myself.

"I am Ursula," the voice from the pool says, offering a watery palm.

"You're fired," Meg says.

"Ha!" Ursula says, and then to me: "Vhy don't ve throw her in?"

"Better not. She's a bit of a wet rag already."

"Suit yourself." Ursula is still wearing the white, beakless, chef's cap. Hair drips from under the brim. It was orange when she got in. Now it's starting to match the nail polish. "She looks angry. Could be dangerous."

"There's a rumour she killed her last husband," I say.

"I don't put much stock in rumours myself." She eyes Meg up and down. "If she did, he undoubtedly deserved it. You should ask vat have you done to earn the anger of a lady so lovely as this." She pinches her nose, sinks under water, pushes off for the other side.

"How 'bout it?" I ask Meg. "Shall we go?"

"I'll call you a cab."

"Come on. Nobody missed me at your party. I was feeling tipsy, so I came in here to work it off. Nobody saw me except Ursula, and she's not going to tell anyone, are you Ursula?"

Ursula is doing sharp quarter turns upside down in the pool. Meg takes her shoes off and sits down.

"I'm the same charming guy I was last night. Just need some food in me. I'll let you drive to the restaurant, okay?" Shit. I'm practically begging.

"If you wanted to sober up, what's that empty bottle doing at your elbow? I'll call you a cab."

"My fault," Ursula says, back at the pool edge. "I drank most of the Heaven Heather. And I am svimming it off."

I put my pants on. "Just don't fire her. Not till you find out where she gets that fabulous green nail polish."

IV

In the restaurant I slide the two C-notes across the table to Meg, giving her the choice again.

"It's not about the money," she says.

"Sure it is. We're not the same type of people, you and I."

"You don't have to work so hard to show it."

"We're from different places is all. The difference is money."

"The difference is you were trying to screw up how I earn my money, while I was trying to help you and Steve make some for yourselves."

"The difference is all you talk about is money while I'm trying to figure out whether I'm worth your attention if I don't have any money."

We leave without eating.

They set up around the corner where you can't see them until it's too late, the traffic too heavy and no place to turn off. A short block past the hospital then a right to climb the escarpment that bisects this city. Around I come and there are the orange cone markers and cruisers, lights flashing, patrolmen, arms arcing, cars and trucks fed left into the lane where they do their business. It's as if I'm their first catch. Crazy I know, but there's that moment you flash to everything you've ever done wrong: the smuggled bottle at the back of the liquor cabinet, the unpaid fines, a knock-down at The Lion you can't remember how it ended. All the shit that makes you think maybe you've finally crossed the line, fucked up enough that it's become worth their while to set this little shindig in your honour.

I look across the front bench to Meg. She says nothing, stares straight out the front glass. I know what's whirling under those blond curls. She's thinking she offered to drive home, offered more than once and maybe I should have listened. I figure we're going to fight, she doesn't get to steer the chevy. Only now Meg is a rock. She says nothing. She's said maybe six syllables since the restaurant.

What are these assholes doing out here anyway? Christmas booze-up is months yet. I'm stopped, a rookie blue at the curb cranking his fist because he wants to talk, so I press the little button to drop the driver's side window.

"Good evening," he says, "we're just doing a seat-belt check and I see you're buckled up and your passenger too, very good, pull up to those gentlemen ahead they're from the Cats they've got a coupon for fifty per cent off tickets for the next home game to thank you for your trouble." The pavement is wet and hisses the way that makes you think you're someplace something might happen.

"I can't believe it."

"It's true. Fifty per cent off. Just pull up to those two guys they're players probably give you an autograph."

"City sets all this up to sell football tickets?"

"We're doing seat-belt checks, sir. The coupon is to thank you for the inconvenience. You don't have to take one. Pull ahead now."

"Sure, you'd have run this seat-belt thingie even if the Cats didn't need help to build attendance. That was just a coincidence. Great the way gears mesh in the universe, eh?"

"Sir, pull ahead now."

"Are you proud to wear that uniform, son? Is this why you took the test?"

He looks behind at the gathering traffic. "One last time. Pull ahead. Now."

"There a problem here?" I recognize the voice. The mirror on my door fills with blue serge and silver metal. I'd known that hand-engraved buckle when it was on a Sam Brown belt. It used to announce that Marion Sherk was on the scene. Now, thirty years and many pounds later, it is more like an announcement of his impending arrival.

"This what you do now, Marion? Shill tickets for the fucking foot-ball club? Christ, I can't believe you're still on the job. What's next month's special? Pots and pans?"

"Get outta here Swan. I shoulda waved you through when I seen ya in the lane."

"We were up for a lot of things, Sherk, you and me, but nothing like this cheese. We never got so low we pulled people over to make them buy shit."

"It's called community-based policing. Not like when you were on the force. I got a computer in the cruiser and everything. I'd show ya, but we're kinda pressed. Do us a favour and fuck off, huh?"

"Suppose I don't? Say I sit here and put a cork in this scam?"

"Suppose I grab you for interfering with an officer?"

"Oh, that'd look good. I still have some friends down at The Spec would like to report that story," I say.

Sherk crouches to my window. "You used up any friends you ever had long ago." He looks across to Meg. "Pardon miss? You say something? Did I just hear you offer to suck this citizen's purple potato for fifty bucks? That's an offer ain't legal, you know. You should take your johns someplace private, talkin' that way. Pretty little thing like you, tell me that ain't what you just said."

Meg turns her gaze from the windshield for the first time since we left the restaurant, and gives Sherk a shine from the finest set of pearlies he's seen outside a tumbler.

"Not tonight I didn't, officer," she says. Damn I could love this woman. Just the tip of her pink tongue runs the back of her lower, reddened lip. "Fifty dollars," she laughs, "Really!"

Meg does me proud. Still, Sherk shouldn't have dragged her into it. Well, I can throw a low shot myself.

Sherk had blown his marriage off, the Missus taking custody, and a big monthly cheque for the kids and the trouble, leaving him with a shitty bachelorette out by the freeway. So I say: "This community-based policing thing could be good, Sherk, if it lets you sell curbside to help put the kids through school. What's your percentage?"

This turns him red, sweat popping out his forehead. The smart thing for me would be to stop now.

"This what you were doing when you gave Bernardo a pass?" I continue.

When they'd finally popped Bernardo for torture/murder/rape, Sherk blurted in the squad room: "Hey, I had that pretty-face in a road-check ages ago. Looked like a pansy so I let him go."

The press got wind and Sherk took a six-week suspension, no pay. So my comment turns him a shade of purple you wouldn't think flesh could be. He belches thirty-three years of unfiltered Export As into my face.

His turd-thick fingers grab my near ear. "You–I'd drag your fat ass out through this window if I thought you'd fit. Shit, I oughtta anyways." He starts to yank.

I throw my fist up and back, knock his arm into the doorpost. Sherk steps away clutching the injured forearm to his gut with his free hand. He stares from four feet back. The eyes are doorways to the soul, but Sherk's brows shade two forbidding entries. He looks about ready to drool. The rookie starts a move, but the veteran waves him back with his uninjured hand. When Sherk comes, he lifts the heel of his right boot and caves the panel of my door. He steps back again, gathers himself, then does the same on the rear door, with a grunt. "Hunh!" He goes around and does both tail lights, and once on the trunk lid for luck. "Hunh-Hunh-Hunh!"

The other cops stop waving traffic. The football players turn around. People climb out of their cars to get a better look as Sherk works his way down the passenger side of my tired chevy. "Hunh-Hunh - Hunh - Hunh," more time between each grunt. Around the front he's breathing hard. He cranks up to take out the front grille like he's kicking for a fifty-yard field goal.

His foot gets stuck. Sherk twists and pulls, suddenly wails like he might have torn something. He hops there for a time, bellowing, one foot stuck in my grille. Caught, like fucking the dog. Eventually three officers come over. Two hold him up while another gently works the angle trying to get Sherk's foot free.

Someone calls an ambulance, though we're hard beside the hospital emergency door. There's some screwing around with gauze, pliers, saws. Meg and I are ring-side through the front windscreen. I twist on the high beams for the sharp, hard light. When they have Sherk sitting on the walk, back up a concrete lamppost and still thundering like a load of steel pipe rolled down the escarpment, one of the blues comes to my window. He surveys the watching crowd, inhales deep and leans in. "Leave now," he says softly. "Make me take you in, I promise a long, slow ride to the station."

I ease the chevy forward. The football players are gone. They haven't come all the way from Pennsylvania or Ohio or wherever, just to sell tickets on the fucking sidewalk.

✦ ✦ ✦

"Want to tell me what that was about?" Meg laughing for the first time this evening.

The low stone wall where Robbie and Liz used to meet stretches out front, separating the parking lot from the drop into the city below. Can't drive a car straight over, though it's been tried. Windows on cars either side of us are steamed, giving the occupants the privacy of curtains.

"Some other time."

"But you know him."

"Sherk? Yeah, of course," I admit. "Never anybody's pal, but I should have let the Bernardo thing go. Wasn't all Sherk's fault." I shift weight to catch her profile. There's a bump on the bridge of her nose I hadn't noticed before, gives it a bit of a hook. City lights dance in her eyes. "We had a description. It wasn't good. Could have been a lot of guys and we didn't have a sure link it was the same guy dragging kids off the street. I mean, these guys don't have fangs. They did, they'd never get close enough to do anyone harm. On the sidewalk they look like you and me." I looked down at the gravy stain on my tie. "Better even."

Cars come and go. People get out to sit on the stone wall to get a better view across the bay and down the lake to Toronto. Others walk out into the darkness on either side of the lot. As the night advances, more visitors stay in their cars. A figure in an overcoat strolls the concrete walk between the cars and the stone wall, stopping to look in the windshields of cars still occupied.

"Bernardo charmed Sherk. He was agreeable, cooperative, even offered to help look. Offered to help look for himself. And Sherk would have thought 'Who's this asshole to help me?' and told Bernardo to get lost. But after, Sherk knew he'd been had. Just another part of the whole thing nobody wants to talk about, except Sherk. His mistake was admitting he'd had Bernardo in the first place. He not only talked, he bragged."

"Is that why he's still working the street? I mean, no offense, but he looks a lot older than you."

"He's there and I'm gone. That got me, I admit, when I saw him in the rear-view tonight. It's a lousy job. It's supposed to be, and Sherk's lousy at it. I don't know what he found makes it worth hanging on to. The Bernardo stuff, that kind of thing kept him from getting promoted. Kissing ass kept him on the force."

"That why you're not?"

She'd like to believe it. I'd like her to believe it. I'd like to believe it myself. "Serve and Protect. Question is, what's worth protecting and who do you have to service to do it?"

Not enough air from the open window to stop the window mist, and it's getting cool. I start the car, direct the increasing engine heat to the front windscreen.

"Sherk wasn't even embarrassed he'd missed Bernardo. Not back then anyway. You notice he had nothing to say about it tonight. Maybe he had no reason to be embarrassed. It's not like shit stopped happening because Bernado was put away. Is there less because he's off the street, or more because of the publicity he got? I don't know. The big silence wrapped around the Bernardo case didn't serve the cop on the beat, I know that. It didn't protect the public. I thought Sherk understood that, but I guess I was wrong. I guess that's why I quit. I didn't give up much."

"Just your pension."

"Part of it. I get by."

She's staring out the windshield. It's getting hot, so I crack my side window. In the car next to me a finger end draws a heart in the mist on the passenger window. Backward initials appear inside the heart, followed by Cupid's arrow.

"Sue-Anne said you quit because your wife died," Meg says.

"She was sick. Then dying. I thought I owed her my time more than I owed it to the force. Anyway, I didn't quit. They pushed me into early retirement, instead of giving me leave. I could have fought it, but that would have been the same as going to work. I was already someplace else." I watch the heart and arrow fade into the window mist. "Don't get illusions. I didn't do her much good either."

"I don't believe that."

"Lady, you don't know shit about me."

"I know you think I killed my husband."

She's pretty. Hair mussed I notice for the first time since the party, but still pretty, and sitting next to me. "No, I don't know that either."

"But you're trying to find out."

"I'm trying to figure out if I care."

The man in the overcoat has worked his way along to stare into the car next to us, the one with the fading heart and arrow. What can he see, I wonder, through the fogged glass? Fumbling bits of pink flesh, bouncing in the rhythm of sex? What?

"You're probably better off with a man who'd prefer chatting with your friends to swimming in an empty swimming pool," I say.

"They're my work, not my friends," Meg says. "I only invited you so you could talk to Big and Leery."

"Lot of good that did."

"When I saw you'd given up, I sent Ursula in to keep you company. I knew she'd look after you. She taught me to swim when I was small."

"You never intended to fire her?"

"A little joke we play."

Overcoat moves in front of our car. Our windscreen's unfogged, so he can see there's nothing more than conversation here. Maybe he just wants to look at Meg.

"So what's this about?" I ask. " I mean us. Why haven't you packed bags yet? You going to take the room at my place or not?"

She gives a little finger wave to overcoat outside. "You're a shit disturber Swanee. That's what your friends call you, isn't it?"

"Friends call me John."

She turns back to me. "I've never dated an ex-cop before."

I roll the chevy's side window all the way down. Cool night air pours in. I call to Overcoat, now peering in our front windscreen: "Go home Frank. Stop bothering people in the park."

"I will not," he says. "Somebody has to do something about the filth that goes on around here; the police certainly don't."

"If they did, you'd have to take up a new hobby."

He sucks wind like the little engine that could. "I've a mind to report you to your superior officer."

They'd get a charge out of it at Central. I consider giving him names, but Meg says: "Should we give him a show?"

"My house is just across the road."

Meg opens her purse, pulls out a red plastic toothbrush. "I know," she says, placing her hand on my thigh. "Is that your motor purring?"

V

At the top of the stairs, Meg turns to the bathroom, flicking on the light but leaving the door open. She gazes at the mirror over the sink, touches her lipstick with the painted nail of the small finger on her right hand, pushes at her hair. Her blond hair. She opens her purse, brings out the toothbrush, scrubs her teeth. When she's done, she puts the brush in the cabinet behind the mirror. Gives me a wink.

A line of light escapes under Steve's door into the dark hallway. Meg knocks.

"Can I come in?"

"N-no."

"Oh. I wanted to tell you, I think you've got your grant from the city."

Rustling behind the door. "Uh, okay. Thanks."

She starts to lean her weight against the hollow panel. "Don't go in," I say, flicking the light switch beside by my bedroom door. "He's all right. Probably thinking about you."

I cross my room, turn on the lamp beside my bed. Meg turns off the switch beside the door and watches while I strip to my boxers and socks. I sit on the side of the bed. My nuts itch. I want to scratch. I scratch.

"I could do without the monkey act. Leave something to my imagination," she says.

I stop.

Okay, I've let myself get distracted. Been years, decades even, since I've had to seduce a woman.

"We don't have to do this tonight. It's only sex," she says.

"That what you told Big and Leery?"

"What?"

"Well, what should I think? I know Big and Leery. Every favour has its price."

"And that price has to be my ass? I think I'll leave now," Meg says.

"Please. I don't want you to leave." What do I want?

I throw dirty clothes from a small, upholstered chair beside my dresser into the closet, sit in the chair, leaving the bed for Meg. Liz had bought me a red silk robe the Christmas before she'd died, size 3X. It had blue paisley thingies, a blue collar and belt. Tonight might have been a good time to get it out of the box, start working on my presentation.

"Did I tell you I was a model?" Meg says.

"I believe it."

"Thanks, but that's not what I mean. I don't have to sleep with the likes of Big and Leery. I've never had to. I know enough men with enough money to support a struggling artist, and companies to write it off as advertising. Men who will donate to Big and Leery's funding scam if I approve the artist who receives the grant. Yeah, Big and Leery want it same as everybody else. But they don't get any, and they don't bring it up as long as I bring them money to skim. The man with the money gets the pleasure of my company at a party of public appreciation. I won't say I've never slept with any of them, but that isn't because I have to. It's my choice who I sleep with."

"I don't have any money."

"I know. But last night you didn't let Sue-Anne boss you around. We went out, places Ham didn't know existed. I had fun. I said earlier you were a shit disturber, but I could be wrong. Maybe you're just a disturbed shit." She stands. "I won't hang around forever waiting to find out which it is."

Hang around? Who in fuck asked you to hang around? Hanging around was your idea for Chrissakes, but I keep this to myself.

"Okay, I'll see you in the morning then," I say. Not the sewing room tonight. Out the door and downstairs to my usual chair, stopping only at the kitchen for the Heaven Heather to help me think. I've known Meg two days and already we've had two fights. All right, first one was my fault, but still, two fucking days?

48

The way she handled Sherk though. And Sue-Anne's crowd. I could watch her do that again and again. Is that what she did with Big and Leery, handle them? Is that what she's doing with me?

If Liz were here I could talk it out with her until I knew. But she's not. What I need is a couple days away from Meg's crowd and putting on airs. Another splash of Heaven Heather. Someplace with real people who don't talk with double meanings. I switch on the stereo, drop the arm on Betty Carter, pour another shot.

Pussy-whipped isn't necessarily bad. If you've got to be whipped, Meg's pussy's the way to have it. Should have sat beside her, given her time, tasted the places behind her ears, long whisps of hair, undressing her slowly, fumbling. It's been so long. Does this betray Liz? Betty Carter's voice fading as I follow into sleep.

"You think I killed Ham," Meg says, arching, taking me into her.

"No," I think.

"Afraid I'll kill you?" my hand up her thigh, feeling only silk skin, the roundness of her, breasts swaying, dipping to my lips.

"Afraid you won't," I answer. "Afraid I'll spend the rest of my life knowing what happens next. I want to be on your conscience. I want to be inside you, wondering if this will be the time, and why, and how." My hands exploring her neck, down her spine, her knees, through sweat-wet crevices. She begins the rhythmic slide, and the bedsprings chorus: "Kill me, kill me, kill me, kill me..."

✦ ✦ ✦

"Where you going?" Meg at the back door as I go down the walk, powered by dog hair. Liquid dog hair. Hair of the dog.

"Holidays. Need some time at The Farm."

Not the same gang every time. I'm only there once or twice each year myself, but there's always some familiar faces with a couple of new guys I'll know before I leave again.

"You might have said."

Said what? That it's you I need the holiday from? I stifle this, still not sure I want it to be true.

"I'm hardly ready. I'm not packed. I..."

I look at those gold curls swirling in the low, early fall light and doubt she was ever not ready for anything. A hook on her nose making her face more beautiful. I lift my gym bag. "Change of underwear and a toothbrush," I say. "You have a toothbrush in the house, I think."

"But look at how I'm dressed, and I don't have clean underwear here," giving me the look, wanting to be coaxed.

"Buy what you need there."

"I've got things to do. I'm supposed to..."

"What makes it a holiday," and I turn, crunch gravel to the chevy. Then stop, turn back. "Like hooky from school."

Five minutes later we're backing out the drive, headed east, car full of cigarette smoke. Bumping off the end of six-lane highway forty minutes later, dropping from the elevated expressway into the never-land of hopeful dreams, left at Coxwell, right at Queen to a place that barely exists anymore. A place of sports and touts, grifters and cons who scamper from rabbit holes the city has forgotten.

"This is The Farm?" she asks as I throw my bag onto the double bed that takes up most of the pastel room we've rented. To the left is a toilet I'll have to stand sideways to piss in. Meg, being perfectly proportioned, will fit easily, even in the undersized tub.

"Nope. This is the Beaches Hotel. The Farm is across the road."

She leans out the window while I enjoy the view. "Old Woodbine?" she asks.

"What's left of it. They've subdivided the track and stables for condos and semis and shit. But you can still lay a few down in the off-track. It's sort of designed to be like under the old grandstand. Just like the old days, long as you didn't actually go track-side in the old days."

"Where do they race?"

"Cambellville, Royal City, New Woodbine, wherever. Piped in by TV, noon to midnight."

"Well, at least I can take the bus home," she says. She's yet to unpack her toothbrush. Keeping her options open.

I take my chrome mickey from my pocket, tilt it to my mouth. We drained it in the chevy. "Have to hit the liquor store. After that, the city is at your feet. We're all right long as we remember which way is up."

One floor to the sidewalk. She looks out the window again.

"The Farm?"

"Come on. It'll be fun."

Part 2

VI

Red lights streak the street gully. A female voice barks orders from a steel box. A crowd. Two cruisers, one with its ass hung out in traffic. A line of cars trying to get around, to get moving and to see at the same time. A third cruiser parked on the sidewalk, nose up the narrow parking lot on the hotel's east side.

"What is it?" Meg asks, zipping her coat.

"I'll see." That's my voice.

Push through the crowd to a strip of yellow tape between the curious and the parking lot.

"Hey, watch it eh?" A male voice. A woman, all glitter, holds on to him, gripping her foot. I've stepped on somebody. "Fuck you."

I ask a blue behind the tape: "What's up?"

"Nothing that won't be at the back of tomorrow's paper." Pushes me away.

"Somebody dead back there." A voice next to me. Cops all over the parking lot, walking in a row from the street, planting little yellow flags on the asphalt. Further in a knot of men in plainclothes huddle. I push out to Meg.

"A murder, maybe. Up by where we parked the chevy. Go down to Java Hut, get us a coffee. I'll get a closer look."

"I'll stay with you."

"No."

She follows me to the hotel's front door.

"I'll tell you what I find out. Get us some coffee. I need coffee."

Her eyes. "I'm not afraid of a few cops."

"I am. Just get the fucking coffee. Please?" Shit.

Something gone. Something we'd planned to do I'd been looking forward to. Gone. She frowns. She nods. She goes.

Down the long, central hallway of the Beaches Hotel to a doorway with EXIT glaring red above. Stairwell. Door opens directly into the parking lot not far from my chevy.

The car looks about ready for Malcolm. I've seen Malcolm this trip, at The Farm, so we've been there, Meg and I. I remember it was Sherk gave the chevy a going-over, last week. Reddish-brown streaks over those dents now, like kids' finger-paint. On the trunk lid, down the rear fender and passenger side doors. That wasn't Sherk. More red on the ground, ending in a puddle still glistening beneath a body under my foot, me stepping from the hotel.

Two gaping grins below my outstretched shoe. Purple snaking beneath the body. White light flashes me blind. Shouting.

I should be away. I should go somewhere, clear my head, should be the fuck away until I can at least remember what happened before the few minutes that put me into this stairwell and opened the door onto this parking lot.

"You. Stay right there."

The head comes back into view, slowly gains colour, the whole scene filling back in around a dot of red light it still hurts to look at. The face askew from the torso, tongue out, licking grit from the asphalt. Another mouth gaping below the chin. I've seen this face, these clothes. Recently. Someone I've met; not an old acquaintance.

The photographer looks up, surprised to see me. I've interrupted him collecting official memories. "Who in fuck're you?" But his lips haven't moved.

Two men behind my car, hands in their pockets. One in a checkered sport jacket, the other in a tan topcoat open over a big belly, shirt white. That's the one. Topcoat shouting my way. Trying to make his down-east, Maritime lilt sound manly.

"Can't nobody see this is a fucking police investigation?" the dick shouts at everyone. I know he's a dick, but I've never seen him before. "Who's minding that door?"

The line of blues hunches in from the street, flagging anything looks out of place in the parking lot. Another bunch I didn't see from the road is diving the hotel's dumpster in the back corner. A blue looks up from a garbage bag. "The manager said it was locked."

"But it's a hotel, am I right?"

The blue nods.

"Then it's a fire exit?"

"He said it was locked, sir."

"Yes, locked to the outside and open from the inside, with a panic bar, in case of an emergency." The blue says nothing. Sport-jacket begins to slip his hands into latex, as the blue line approaches from the street.

"Put some barrier tape across that bloody door," Topcoat yells. "On the inside. Post a man if necessary. You," pointing to me, "wait right there."

Sport-jacket goes through the dead man's pockets. He lays hands on the shoulders, points a medic to take the feet. Together they roll the corpse, the head moving but not turning, Sports-jacket's face twisting away. Guts spill onto the asphalt, like fish slopping from a net. Shit stink rises like a departing soul.

I back into the stairwell, gag, head for the hallway. The door opens. Topcoat walks into me.

"I told you to wait. Who in fuck do you think you are?"

I haven't words. He shoves, shoves again. I can't get round him.

"Name is Swan. John Swan. A room here, at this hotel." Dig in my pocket. There's a key. Number 2C.

"That supposed to impress me? Give me five minutes, I could buy three sets of keys for this fuck-pad in the first booze-can I find."

"Ask, ask the manager."

"Rooms rent here by the hour, asshole. Management isn't credible to back up a small car."

That's why I never bring anything to the Beaches Hotel worth stealing. A change of underwear and two bottles of Heaven Heather in the half-moon gym bag packed for the room upstairs. "Come here for the races, since there was a real track. Come back now and again to the off-track, you know, see old friends."

Nothing worth stealing. Is that why I've brought Meg? That was a mistake. Except it was her wanted to come, I remember. At least I think I remember.

"The fuck you from?"

I tell him. Tell him I was on the force back home. My knees go wobbly. Shit, can't be he bothers me that much. Take a grip on the stair railing. Maybe something I ate. Can't remember what.

Topcoat doesn't wear a Bogie trench. No belts or straps. No fedora. Not even Columbo crumpled. Nothing special about it. Brown shoes and a blue suit. "Ex-cop," he says. The idea makes his lips curl. His eyes squint, go flat. He rubs them with his right hand. "What kind of friends could a piece of shit like you keep here in Toronto?" he asks.

"Don't think I deserved that," I tell Meg later in the Java Hut, over my third coffee, getting my head clear. And now I remember her leaning out our room window in the hotel. What have I done since then?

"I just left the off-track across the road," I tell Topcoat. "Saw the commotion here at the hotel. Came out to see what it's about. Staying here at the hotel."

"Being a former police detective yourself, you just naturally want to be helpful."

"Something like that." I burp.

"A fucking wino ex-dick from the Hammer. Why do I feel my load just got heavier, not lighter?"

I make to leave. "You don't want what I've got, that's fine," I say. Need to sit somewhere.

He blocks. "Not so fast asshole." He smiles. He's not good at sincerity. "Render us your assistance."

There are six cars in the lot. Mine is the only one smeared with blood. They'll check ownership and interview all the drivers anyway. No point trying to duck it.

"Okay. First," I say, "the brown chevy just outside the door? Belongs to me."

"That's it? There's prints all over it. When did you last wash that thing?"

I have to think. "1998."

"That's all you know about the mess out there?"

"Well, it's a V8 automatic with power steering and brakes..."

"Heh heh. A little chuckle at my expense. That's fine. I've a sense of humour too. How about we go to division? You can tell me more funnies and I'll tell you some of mine."

"Sure. We can compare attitudes."

"So you admit you had an attitude?" Meg says later in the coffee shop.

"I get attitude I give it back. Otherwise I'm the charmer you know and are learning to love." She doesn't look convinced. "I might have said something about how he wouldn't have got further than women's auxiliary in any city with real crime."

Meg rolls her eyes. "What then?"

"He turned red."

"You don't think that dead fucker outside is real enough?" Topcoat asks.

I don't think he's looking for an answer. His right hand slides along his belt to his back, a move I recognize. He's reaching for his tools. I step in, put my arms around him. It brings us beak to beak. He's had fish for dinner. Breakfast too, by the smell of his breath.

"One shout from me and ten men come through that door," he says, nodding toward the one at the end of the hall. I doubt he can shout loud enough to be heard above the noise on the other side of the steel fire door.

"Even I could tell you it's not a good idea to hug a cop," Meg points out, "especially when he's on duty. Is this the way Topcoat would describe events?"

"Not his story," I answer, gulping my coffee. "In his story," I add, "I doubt he insults the chevy. Anyway, I only held him to keep him from slugging me. I was going to explain, find an alibi, prove we were on the same side, me willing to cooperate."

"Uh-huh. How'd you get that bruise?"

"Don't remember. I do remember it was hot in the hallway. Could've been the smell of his morning kippers, or the sight of the body got to me. Don't know which, but my stomach heaved."

"You threw up?"

"You remember what I had for dinner? That might've done it."

She looks at my shirt. "You puked on a cop, a detective?"

"Mostly over his shoulder. Wouldn't have been so bad if he hadn't been squirming. None would have gone down his collar then. I was sweating and my legs went rubber, so I couldn't let go of him until I was empty."

"So somebody thumped you and you stopped giving them wiseass."

"What do you mean by that?"

"You can't have hit back. They wouldn't have let you go if you had." I think she's relieved.

"Topcoat tried a couple kicks. I think mostly he just wanted away and out of his coat. Probably didn't want his partner to see him like that. I might have said I was sorry. Maybe not."

She shakes her head. "Doesn't sound like you. What *did* you tell him?"

I lift both palms. "Past couple days are a bit out of focus. Made some stuff up. One thing, did I mention? I must have."

"What?"

"The body in the parking lot, the dead guy. That was Toby."

VII

"I need your help, Meg. I do know somebody named Toby, don't I?"

"We met him at The Farm, remember, he was looking for his daughter? We saw him, maybe three times. We met him Friday and he was looking for his daughter Gretchen. Then Saturday morning, he had found her. At some point on Saturday night we found out he'd lost her again. I thought he was an old friend of yours."

I squint to show Meg I'm thinking hard. Makes my head hurt.

"I don't think so. I mean, I recognized him lying on the ground, so I know I knew him, but if I knew him before this trip, I'd remember him like I remember you." I take the mickey from my pocket, aim it at my fresh tea. Meg reaches, lays a hand on mine before I pour.

"Maybe you're right," I say, put the lid back on.

She hadn't brought coffee to the hotel like I asked. I had to track her to the Java Hut. She took my jacket soon as I came in, bought soda water and started dabbing with paper napkins. I drank half the cup to rinse the taste from my mouth. Then started on the coffee. Now tea.

She frowns. "How much do you remember?"

"I remember some things, some things I'll work out. They'll come back if they're important. Always do." It's not a headache exactly. Just the feeling one is near, sitting on my shoulders, waiting for the right moment. "Faster if you help me."

"You'll want these," I'd said, dangling my keys before Topcoat's nose as evidence of cooperation.

"Too bad. Now the lab boys won't need to pop a window."

"When do I get it back?" I knew better than to ask.

He smiled. "Depends what we find to link you to the vic."

There's nothing to find, but I'm sure he'd be the type to find it, I told him. The bloom had gone off our relationship.

I tell Meg: "I'd like maybe to get things sorted because he'll be asking me more questions soon."

"Do you remember why we came to Toronto?"

"I remember you starting a fight in The Onion."

"There were men fighting in The Onion. You were fighting in The Onion. Not me."

"Yeah. All the same, it was you started it."

✦ ✦ ✦

We'd gone to the liquor store first, to pick up a couple of mickeys. One went in my jacket pocket, the other in Meg's purse. Then past a vacant lot, past the little pizzeria rumoured to be a mob front. Two fried chicken joints on the same block, one independent and one a chain. I stepped into a narrow alley, pulled Meg behind, unscrewed my flask. We swigged. Then we kissed, long and slow. I tasted the Heaven Heather on her tongue. A long pull on the flask for me and we were off again. A red light stopped us on the corner outside Java Hut.

"There's a cop shop up that way," I pointed north, "two, three blocks."

She put her right hand on my chest. "Won't you keep me safe?"

"I'm warning you, not directing you."

The light changed. I took her arm, helped her over the trolley tracks curving through the intersection. Another half block brought us to The Onion Chop House. It was still early. A mob would soon form on the sidewalk waiting to get in, while another spread across the linoleum just inside the door, blocking the windows. A notice taped to the inside of the glass beside a menu said The Onion would soon move to fancier digs two doors west. Meg read the menu. The restaurant was tiny, no more than a half dozen Formica-topped tables and maybe eight stools along the counter. The walls were covered with signs advertising the same menu in several different type sizes: four cuts of steak, pork chops, burgers, breakfast. We took a booth on the left.

The waitress came, lifted dirty dishes from our table and wiped the plastic with a damp, grey cloth. "Something to drink?" she asked, her dress faded splotchy green.

"Beer," I said.

"Draft?"

I nodded.

"Cup of tea," Meg said. She was still deciding. Not the menu, the restaurant. Meanwhile, she'd have her water boiled.

A man entered wearing a Chicago Blackhawks jersey. He stood at the counter with men who'd thrown friendly abuse and balled napkins his way as he'd crossed the room. They wore Leafs jerseys. Drinks arrived. I poured some of my flask into my beer, raised my head to Meg before putting the lid back on. Maybe she didn't know how well Heaven Heather goes with tea.

"Sort of like Long Island Ice Tea," I suggested, "without the ice."

She shook her head. "Without Long Island," she said.

Two students took the booth between us and the window. No sooner had they sat than they went back outside to help a street vet weaving the patch of the sidewalk past the restaurant, twice falling against parked cars for two-minute time outs.

I ordered the 12oz. tenderloin, medium rare. Meg asked if she could get a salad and the waitress said sure, but I put a hold on it. "Try the tenderloin," I said to her, so she ordered the 8 oz., with a salad side.

The waitress nodded. "How you want it?"

"Medium rare."

"Anything else?" We shook our heads. "Onions? Mushrooms?"

"Mushrooms," I said, "and another beer." Meg hadn't touched her tea.

"Cocktail?" I asked.

"Rye and soda," she said. That's my girl.

The kids came back from helping the drunk. I'd missed what they did with him. Meantime their booth had been taken.

My beer came, and Meg's rye. This is how you wait tables. No phony smiles and no phony bread smell pumped into the room. This place smelled like a real restaurant should: a cross of grease, onions and Lysol.

Another trip, the waitress brought a plate stacked with buttered bread slices, and our fried mushrooms. Then the steaks, thick as my wrist. I ordered another beer. Meg's drink was only half gone, not that I was counting. We tucked in.

"Breakfast anything like this?" Meg asked, laying down her fork with a couple of ounces still to go. She was on her second rye then, too.

"No, but it's damned good just the same. To be honest," I admitted, "the bread's nothing special."

I pointed to a piece on the side of her plate, one bite gone. "And the slices of raw onion and tomato," she said.

"Yeah? I thought they were a nice touch."

"Mashed potatoes are creamy," we agreed, and ordered tea for both of us. Tea's fine, long as you don't have to go to all the trouble of fixing it yourself.

We waived dessert. "Couldn't," Meg said, "stuffed," and got the bill. A bit of the flask went into the tea. I paid with the refills. "That's fine," I told the waitress.

She did a quick count. "Thanks, dear. Come again."

I looked at Meg, raised both my brows. She warmed her hands around her cup and smiled. Then she looked past me down the narrow room, toward the chop house counter.

"You know those men at the bar?" she asked. "They keep looking at us."

I twisted round to see the two Maple Leafs jerseys turned our way. The guy wearing Blackhawk colours grinned into his beer. I shrugged, shook my head.

"Washroom?" Meg asked me, wiping her mouth with a napkin.

"Down the back on the right," I told her.

She walked slowly, stopped to say something to the Blackhawk jersey. I couldn't hear what, but he liked it, laughed while she said something to the closest Maple Leaf jersey. He liked it too. Meg shoved off, walked slowly to the john.

They looked me over while she was in there, sizing me up. The place was full now. When she came out, Blackhawk jersey put his arm around her waist. She leaned into him, put her free arm around Leaf jersey. They joshed and jostled, then Meg slapped Blackhawk. She shifted to Leaf jersey. His back was to me. Leaf Number Two was on his near side, one eye for his buddies, the other for me. Blackhawk scowled, pushed Leaf Number One, sending Meg butt first into somebody's creamy mashed potatoes. Leaf Number One dove into

Blackhawk and Blackhawk pawed Leaf One's jersey up his back and over his head. Leaf Two thought he saw his opening. He helped Meg steady to her feet, took her arm and a step toward the door. That's when I cold-cocked him.

He stood there, dumbstruck, eyes like dinner plates and the blood from his broken nose starting down his face into his collar. He didn't howl until I hit him again, same spot, right on the button. Then he brought his hands up to cover his face, the blood really flowing now and tears glistening his eyes.

His buddies caught on that the action had shifted, left off their hug and shove match to help out. I pulled Meg behind me, kicked Leaf Two's right knee out from the inside. He went down, and his buddies fell over him trying to get at me. They sprawled on the floor as we backed to the doorway. I picked up Meg's jacket from our booth on the way. The crowd around the door parted to let us through.

"I thought it was customary to kick a man in the testicles," Meg said.

"He'll remember me longer with the ligaments in his knee popped."

"Did you break his nose?"

"Second punch, if not the first."

It struck me she was savouring the details. Having started the fight, or the chain of events that led to it, she wanted to see how I'd finish it. I checked over my shoulder in case the jerseys followed us out, but they were hockey bullies, not brawlers, and knew enough to stay down, take what sympathy they could get from the other Friday night regulars. I felt good, alive. Something to remember. That was Meg's doing, and I'll remember being with her when it happened, and how good it felt.

Remembering this, I knew I'd eventually recall the next twenty-four hours. Because Meg had been there, all would come back to me. For twenty-five years give or take, my job had been to fill in the details of what happened and when. Meg made that seem worth doing again. So I let her decide what we'd do next.

VIII

"Go back to your last complete memory. Start there," Meg advises me.

"After The Onion?"

"Go back to your last complete memory."

"Why?"

They keep things bright and clean in Java Hut, like it's a safe haven from the darkness outside. A door swings open behind the counter and a man wearing a white T-shirt, white pants, a white apron, enters. He carries a silver wire rack. His arms are powdered with white flour, spotted by the sweat dropping from his forehead. The tray slides into a display case behind the counter. Sandwiches are on display, probably from the previous day. The thought catches at the back of my throat.

"It's a way to remember. Don't wait for it all before you start. Just begin with what you remember and tell it like a story and it'll keep coming. You'll see. Things you couldn't remember if you just concentrated on them. You'll see."

Meg lights a cigarette. The ash grows long. She lets it drop into my styrofoam cup.

"I was just thinking, what happened to the red nightie we bought this afternoon?"

"That you remember," Meg says.

"Of course."

+ + +

We strolled the shopping strip a few blocks east of The Farm. Meg browsed a bookstore for almost an hour, before buying a book by Walter Mosely. I picked up a newspaper, so as not to be one-upped in the intellectual department. I'd taken her through Kew Park, around the baseball diamond, down to the beach that gives the neighbourhood its name, then back through the shaded, house-wedged streets. After the bookstore she ducked into a place that sells ladies' underwear, holding up stuff and asking me what I thought, the young salesgirl standing at her elbow.

The clerk was dressed slick, black and shiny, her getup revealing arcs of dark brown above her nipples. Her nails and lips were black, her short hair painted red. When she smiled, silver flashed on her tongue. Gave me something to think about while Meg finally selected. I hoped an early night at The Farm, or maybe skip it altogether.

And there it is, just like Meg said. We were going to The Farm later. But what day was this, what time?

"I'll pay for that," I said when we approached the counter.

"Why? Think it's for you?" Meg asked.

"How much?" to the salesgirl.

"Eighty-six twenty with tax," she said. I blinked. "Fifty per cent off a Slammo vibrator with all purchases over thirty dollars," she added. She held an eight-inch, fluorescent blue cock under my nose. "This week's special."

Is this something Meg would like? I wondered. I shouldn't have started thinking again. Took way too long.

The clerk was saying: "It's a customer favourite. Bring it back for exchange if you're not one hundred percent satisfied."

"Got one already," Meg said, giving me a pat on the crotch. "Only I can't seem to find the off switch."

"There isn't one," I told her. "You're supposed to wear it out." I smiled for the salesgirl, but it felt like the smile of a dirty old man.

Outside, in cool air and on solid concrete again. Light falling, shops starting to close, folding my wallet, so I must have finished the buy. My feet hurt and I was hungry but Meg had me thinking I could handle another couple hours of chick stuff if it meant tonight's the night. We'd both been too tired the night before. The walk, the trip down, the whole day. I probably fell asleep before she did.

She took my arm and pulled me at a half run, laughing, weaving through traffic across the road. Outside the doorway of a pub taking up half the block, she kissed me hard and long, bending one leg back from the knee like in the movies. She gave me another little squeeze, laid a hand on my chest.

"I'm going to see if they've got any real underwear in that store down the block. Go have a beer and think about what we'll do for dinner," she said. "Give The Onion a rest."

✦ ✦ ✦

"The Onion again," I say. "You didn't want to go there for some reason."

We shift our feet so the Java Hut counterman can wash the floor under our table. If it bothers him that we're nursing the tea, he doesn't let on. Maybe it gives him time to study for his bar exams.

"If we didn't go to The Onion this can't have been Friday."

Meg says, "We had dinner someplace better."

I see a dining room, dark wood. "Nigel was there, with somebody you know."

"Nigel?" she asks.

"I mean Neville, with somebody tall, dark hair going silver at the edges."

"I never saw them."

"What about the red nightie? Where's it at now?"

"It's after four in the morning. Aren't you tired?"

I'm nearly dead, and worse now she's asked. We get up and shuffle toward the coffee shop door.

"Keep talking," she says. "But this time start when we left The Onion. Just tell the story, one thing after the other as it comes to mind."

"Why don't you just tell me?"

"I want to see how you put it together. You're the detective, right? How did you figure out what went down when you were on the job?"

"People told me."

Grey dawn. Meg and I outside the hotel. Beside it is an empty place where my chevy used to be.

In our room Meg announces, "I'm going to have a shower. You understand?" She heads for the loo. "A long, hot shower. For as long as the hot water holds up. You do what you like. You want to sit around dreaming of a red nightie go right ahead, but I'll be in the next room. Steamy. Naked."

I sit on the end of the bed, pretending to think it over. On the one hand, I don't want to act like it's the only thing on my mind. On the other hand, it's been on my mind since that first night with Sue-Anne and Robbie, and I'm pretty sure nothing's happened like that yet.

I did buy the red nightie today. Actually, it was yesterday. We're well into Sunday now. How do I know that? Saturday I bought the nightie because things hadn't worked out right Friday night. Why?

I rise, open the bathroom door. Steam pours out, tendrils weighting my legs. I feel my way to the small tub where Meg stands. She's pink. Her flesh squeaks as it folds into mine. There isn't room for us both in the tub. I wash her from outside, rinsing her again and again with a stream of soaps, shampoos, lotions and rinses supplied in little packets by the hotel, round globs of flesh slipping through my hands.

"Didn't take you long," Liz says. She's sitting on the toilet seat, right leg over the left like she always did, leaning forward, unlit cigarette.

Meg disappears down the drain along with the soap, the suds, the steam. If I've got to dream this crap I'd at least like to get to the end.

Or I should start dreaming something else. Toby's face swims into view. I've met him three times, I'm sure. The last time he was dead, in the hotel parking lot. The first time was Friday night. He came crashing into The Farm about ten.

"Anybody see Gretch?" He didn't sit. Didn't even look for a chair.

Heads shook, silently, watching the overhead TV screens. The eleventh had started at Royal City.

"I don't know what to do. She was supposed to be here by six, seven at the latest. Sure you ain't seen her? What time you get here?"

"Who?" Neville asked.

"Gretchen, my daughter Gretchen. I get her one weekend a month. This is my weekend."

Neville and his buddy Cecil are from the aqua-blue Caribbean, and seldom seen apart. Soon as he spotted Meg and I coming into the room, Cecil's smile broadened. Good to see old friends. But Cecil quickly scrounged a seat for Meg, held it while she sat. Maybe the smile was for Meg. Good to meet new friends too, especially when they look like Meg.

I had to find my own chair, then opened the racing form I'd bought on the way in. "Anything good tonight?"

An old Chinese guy passed by our table, wearing a grey fedora and shuffling along on blue slippers. He nodded hello to no one in particular. Meg nodded back.

Cecil said "You got de Campbellville program. Nothing good can happen to you dere, man. Bet two dollar, win two-fifty back. Cecil say you not a lucky man." And he laid one long arm across the back of the chair he'd brought for Meg.

Neville is woolly with a multicoloured knit cap. He's a watcher, seldom speaks even when spoken to. Cecil usually has a grin and a tan baseball cap, beak to the front at his own, off-beat angle. He leaned to Meg again, almost putting his nose in her hair. "Toby got the job steering a diaper truck around the city. You sit next to him, you can sniff how he earn his betting money."

Toby heard Cecil laugh. "You think it's funny? Years I spent paying some shark, now I've lost her already it's maybe her third visit."

Until this moment, I didn't know this guy. Toby is a skinny little pecker. Ask me, he's too old to be lugging bags of wet diapers around Toronto, but maybe the laundry company is desperate to keep whoever will do the job.

"How Cecil supposed to know her, man? Cecil don't know no Gretchens."

The Chinese guy came by again. Maybe has a thimble for a bladder.

"I showed you pictures. You remember. Gretchen?"

"We remember," this was Neville, "but your pictures were of a little girl. She must be, how old now? Fifteen?" Toby nodded. "Haven't seen any little girls here tonight, and we've been here since half past five. 'Course, we haven't been watching for her neither."

"Why you think Gretchen come in here?" Cecil asked after Toby started whining again.

"Have you phoned her mother? Maybe she missed her bus." Neville.

"I did, I did. No answer. I've been everywhere I ever took her before, looking, thinking maybe she got mixed up and thinks I said meet her somewheres else. I'm pretty positive we said come to my apartment, but I don't know and I've been down to the bus depot. Nobody's seen her. This was the last place I could think."

Wally jiggled over to our table. "You guys need anything?"

Wally's been a fixture at The Farm long as I've been going, back when it was a real racetrack. He'd worked his way up to the club house. Now he was slinging beer for off-track peasantry. He made sure customers knew he was slumming, taking his time pushing off from his corner to jiggle over in his crisp, white, short-sleeved shirt. He focused watery eyes baggy as his black trousers, and sucked his gums while we came to a decision.

I selected our first round. "Blue, Molsons."

Wally nodded. Meg agreed. Cecil and Neville already had two half-drained bottles.

"Two," Wally said and minced way.

"What I'll do," Toby said, "I'll stay for the twelfth and see if she comes in." He pulled coins from his pocket, along with the thin lining, and counted out toonies.

"You should go home," Neville said. "That's where she's most likely to come looking for you. Keep phoning her Mama. They're probably messing with you, took her to some fancy resort for a weekend just to screw you around because you won visitations. They'll want to see what you do about it, but you should keep phoning in case."

"Shouldn't someone phone the police?" Meg said.

"I'll just put something on the twelfth while I'm waiting," Toby said.

"Why don't you call the police?" Meg asked again.

"He don't want his baby girl feeling no long finger of the law, is why he don't call no police," Cecil answered.

"What's that mean?" Meg.

"Cops strip search everyone they pull in," I answered Meg. "Do a cavity search when they feel the need, which turns out is nearly always."

Neville leaned forward, put his hand over the change Toby was counting at the table edge. "Go home. She comes here, we send her straight over."

"But this is a missing kid," Meg said. "She's not suspected of any-thing. Is she?"

SAP

I answered. "Would you risk it if it was your kid? If you weren't certain what the kid was up to? Or would you leave it a couple hours, hoping for the best?"

"Go home," Neville repeated to Toby.

Toby did a small shudder. He didn't look up. "Right. That's what I should do. She's probably there now, sitting on the steps, waiting to get in." Neville lifted his hand and Toby scooped his change. "You know, it's just I gotta work in the morning, I won't hardly get any time with her as it is. Thanks."

"It'll be fine, just part of the process. You'll see."

Then the Chinese guy again.

"Anybody know this character?" I asked. "What can we do for you pal?" But he kept going, head bobbing like he was licking ass.

When Wally came back, he dropped two Labatt Blues on our table. "All out of Molsons," he said, which has been true for at least fifteen years, when Wally worked the old club lounge. The bar at The Farm boasts eight brands, all the same but for the labels. I waved a twenty at Wally and waited while he made a show of getting change. He earned a loonie for his efforts.

Crouch, young guy, lumberjack shirt, bandana, black fingerless gloves, rolled his wheelchair to an empty side of the table. He scratched a day old beard, said "Rickards," at Wally.

Wally shook his head.

"Honey Brown? Bass? Cream Ale? Anything decent at all?"

Wally's head kept wagging. "Down the street," he said, "you want to put on the lah-de-dah."

"Think I wouldn't if I could? You wouldn't see me again if I could find one place where the doors are wide enough for a wheelchair, or the tables aren't all jammed up."

Cecil put his nose in Meg's ear, said: "Or they didn't already throw his ass out."

"Fuck you," Crouch said, to anyone who could hear. "The usual piss water then." But Wally waited. "Okay. Carlsberg. Please," Crouch added, smiling sweetly until Wally moved. "Prick."

"What's the matter with Carlsberg?" Meg asked Crouch.

"At five-fifty a bottle?"

"Yeah," Cecil observed, "be sorry for any man have to do his serious drinking here." He took a long swallow from his own, and

72

looked at Crouch. "Unless he on disability and get the government to pay."

"I don't need your pity," Crouch said to Cecil, "I just need you to sell me something better."

"Why you say that to me, eh? You think because Cecil's black he sell some kind of shit man? That some kind of racist thing you telling Cecil?"

Crouch looked away. Cecil leaned toward Meg again. "He like that till he get some juice into him. Then he be just fine, you see."

"Next round's on me, then," Meg offered and soon we were all pals.

Meg getting this attention made me realize how few women there usually are in The Farm. Less than ten, counting the two security guards and the one selling track programs. Another thing: butt-suckers make up most of the clientele, but get a third of the space in a separate badly ventilated room. Open the door to the smokers' room and a cloud billows out.

I put a couple to win on some races, watched each race from my seat and earned nothing. Meg and Cecil jumped up to cheer their horses on. He bet both Campbellville and Royal City. Pretty soon, so did Meg. It looked like fun.

Crouch had some story about Toronto cops testing the use of helicopters to patrol the city. "Guy steals a new Caddy from the dealer on Bay Street, right? He's not overly quick. It's loaded, has that global positioning bullshit. Soon as they learn the car's gone, the cops track it by satellite. Guy's joyriding north of the city. When he comes back in town, the cops have the chopper in the air, waiting. Now they track him that way. Do I gotta tell all the stories and buy my own beer too?"

Wally took our order, my round again. Meg and Cecil moved under the TV screen.

Crouch started up again: "They got their eye-in-the-sky ka-thunking away, and they block the road ahead of the Caddy. Except the guy figures to smash right through. Hey, he watches TV, right? Totals the Caddy, a couple of cruisers, sideswipes a row of cars and smashes into a school bus. When they finish beating the shit out of this guy, the cops go on TV and say what a big success the 'copter was. Christ, they must want those things bad. I mean, wouldn't it have been cheaper just to give the guy the fucking Caddy?"

"Police need the tools," Neville said, "they're going to do the job." He's already spoken as much tonight as I usually hear in three visits to The Farm.

"If I win tonight," Crouch said, "I'm gonna buy them one of the navy's used Sea Kings. One hour in the air for every ninety in service. That way they won't wake me up every night going thwacka-thwacka."

I heard Meg's voice rise under the TV screen, hands fisted, her horse moving up in the pack. Cecil's hand moved down her back.

Wally came back with more beer. I swallowed a long draft, spiced my bottle from the mickey.

Meg won again, applauding beneath the TV screen as Cecil put his arm round her and planted a kiss. Meg pulled back, then stepped in. Cecil's thigh slid between hers.

They returned, sat down, Cecil next to me, finishing a sentence for Meg "...you never go back."

Enough of this shit. I grabbed his collar. "I ever treat *you* this way?"

Cecil's eyes came slowly round to me, watching for my next move. "What way is that?"

I had the hotel room key in my fist, the jagged edge exposed between fingers. He was younger and faster than me. I'd have to go first and hard, catch him while he thought about it. No other way to make it come out in my favour. "Hustle your date from under you?"

Meg: "What exactly do you mean by that?" I'd heard that tone back at The Onion, knew she'd be frowning, her brow wrinkled but eyes glistening.

Neville's voice came next, measured, dropping the air pressure in the room: "The answer is no, Cecil. He never behaved the way you're behaving. Neither have I."

Looking at it now, I realize it was more than a warning. All my other trips to The Farm, Cecil had never had eyes for anyone but Neville. I'd never guessed he went both ways. Of course, he'd never laid eyes on Meg before.

Not that I did much thinking about it then. Friday night, after The Onion, and already I was getting a sense of what Meg liked. So I swung.

Cecil pulled back and turned enough to dodge the force. Crouch wheeled back from the table. Cecil's near hand came out of his pocket, but he didn't bring it, not yet. He moved slow, let me see his smile fade, his eyes deaden on me as a ragged red line oozed up on the black of his jaw and neck. He watched me, but answered Neville. "You right. Swanee never treat Cecil this way before."

Over at the bar, Wally had his hand on the phone, eyes casting the room for security staff.

Neville: "We're done here."

Cecil's eyes still on mine, left hand down and back, right hand lightly on Meg's thigh. "What you think Swanee, we done here?"

Neville hissed: "We don't want attention. Not now. I say we're done. Take me home."

The left arm relaxed, the right withdrew, but the eyes stayed. "Okay then. Done for now. Cecil's apologies to the pretty lady."

Meg handed him a tissue dredged from her purse.

"Cecil look forward to seeing you again. And you too, Swanee."

Neville and Cecil left, taking the warmth of the room with them. Outside the glass doorway, Neville stopped to speak to the old Chinese guy.

IX

Meg's not in the room when I wake. Gone for breakfast, maybe. I see her toothbrush beside the sink as I wash. The paper I bought sits on the dresser, unopened. I'm hoping this is Sunday, that it's just one day I'm trying to piece together again. I should slip across to The Farm, tell them about Toby if they haven't heard already. Won't take long.

Five minutes to the one o'clock opening, a dozen punters already mill outside, eager for the thrill of losing. This includes the old Chinese guy, exchanging vowels with an equally old Chinese woman, probably his wife. She's a smiler too. I remember him from Friday night. Up the street, Ivan the Russian single-handedly supports The Farm's long front wall with his lanky frame. He speaks English, so I give him the news instead.

"Da," he says, nodding.

The dream at the off-track is the same as it was at the rail: win enough to quit taking orders from some shit-for-brains boss forty, fifty, sixty hours a week. Enough to get out from under the boredom of operating small garages, or laundries, or fly-specked variety stores on slow side streets. Enough to stop waiting on the dole, shifting apartments, or low-paying jobs for cash at the end of each shift. No more Shylock to come creeping Monday mornings mealy-mouthing promises. What's won is the rush of adrenaline at the wire and the company of people who suffer the same defeats.

A sucking noise at my side.

"What's this then?" Wally in a blue windbreaker, feet splayed flat-footed on the pavement, lunch-bag under one arm, working a toothpick around his gums. Wally who waits tables at The Farm bar. I don't want to think about what Wally dreams.

"Toby's dead. Murdered in the Beaches Hotel parking lot."

He shakes his head. "Helluva way to settle custody, huh."

"Seems a bit extreme," I say. "Murder someone to avoid a custody battle?"

"You wouldn't think so if you knew the kid's mother."

We don't usually notice Wally unless he's slow with the beer. He has my attention now.

"You know the kid's mother?"

"Sure, she practically grew up around the old track. Pretty thing, too. Her folks owned stock, some of 'em decent runners in the old days. Club members, they were, but a kid gets a thing for horses, you know how it goes, she hits puberty an' starts running from one bad habit to the next."

"What bad habits exactly?"

"It all starts with sex, I say." Wally checks out the street in both directions, casts his eyes skyward for inspiration. "It's the stallions. I seen it hundreds a times. Show a young girl a length of horse-cock when she's at that stage of life, she'll never settle. Back before they closed the track I usta try and warn management. If they're gonna let young girls in the stables, geld the stallions. All of 'em. Valerie was jail bait."

"Toby took it?"

"He was a groom back then. Ten years older'n Valerie at least, but skinny enough to show it off in a pair of tight jeans. Wasn't any smarter then than now, no disrespect intended. Brushing horse sweat is a skill like any other, except they don't call it a brain-drain when one of those guys heads for Kentucky. Anyway, next thing Toby and Valerie are gettin' hitched and suddenly, here's Gretchen."

"Only it didn't last," I say.

He nods. "Five years. Give Toby credit, he tried to make it work. He was a drunk, but, you know, there's things worse than beer to hitch your life to." He pours his watery grin, the lower lip dipping precariously to one side. "Gettin' over Val was the first part of Toby cleanin' up."

"Not the other way round?"

"Hell no. Toby could see it was no good for the kid, so he took up the twelve-step, no help from Val. He had to leave her if he was gonna change his act. Don't waste your sympathy on Val. She landed on her pretty tootsies all right, married some guy able to support her nasty habits."

The grin again. "Her family had the money, so Val and Gretchen went with them. They married Valerie off to some guy wouldn't embarrass them slurping champagne cocktails in the Club Lounge. Fella in real estate, name of Cartwright. Val didn't pay Gretchen any more attention than before, only now that's the son-in-law's problem. That's the rich for ya. Son of a bitch, eh?"

A light releases traffic half a block up Queen Street. I slap a hand on Wally's shoulder, wait for streetcar noise to pass.

"You don't miss much."

The loopy grin works overtime. "There's more to fetching beer than you might think. I been working here a long time." Wally taps the side of his head with a soft finger. "I hear things. People say 'em to me or in front of me. I got bursitis from people cryin' on this shoulder." He rotates the arm for emphasis.

"Only if you overheard Toby, he can't have gone teetotal."

Wally shakes that off. "Ice-tea, to be exact. I serve him myself."

"But why's he sipping it at The Farm? He a heavy bettor?"

"Not as long as he stayed away from the track. Except that was Toby's life." The grin deepened, a dribble descending from one corner. "Tell you another thing," he said. "Toby worked for Neville."

"Doing what?"

"The diaper service. Neville owns it. There's more to him than meets the eye. You bet."

The track was Toby's life, only I'd never met him at The Farm until this weekend. "How could Toby afford a drawn-out, legal battle for visitation on a delivery-man's wages?"

"It wasn't just for visitation either. He was after custody—so he said—but maybe he was hoping Val's rich relatives would have to pay him support. You ask me that'd probably be more than Neville pays him to truck around baby shit all day."

"How much more? I mean, what's at stake here? Who is Val's family?"

"You ought to know. Val's an O'Keefe. The old man lives near you, I think. That town other side of you?"

"Ancaster?"

"That's the one. O'Keefe's the type never does nothing by himself. Everything is 'We done this' and 'We done that'. I bumped into him a few months back coming out of the showroom house at the development they're building down here now the track's gone. Couldn't believe it. All the years I carried his mint juleps, this is the first time I seen his loafers scrape pavement. Asked him if he was thinking of buying a house and he said 'we' was checking to see the son-in-law had everything under control. The kid's company handles sales. O'Keefe and his pals from the track club are behind the whole thing, which is probably why O'Keefe married Valerie off to the real-estate guy in the first place, seeing the writing on the wall back when and wanting to keep the profits in the family. You can see O'Keefe's no big fan of moss."

I flash to the silver-haired man taking Meg's arm at her auntie's fundraiser. And another man, sitting with Neville at that Beaches pub. Was that yesterday? They're not the same men, but similar in style, a way of moving, like the world is theirs.

"This Val had all the money and family, so what did Toby have as grounds for custody?"

Wally shakes his head. "Beats me. He said Gretchen wasn't being looked after, that she was hanging with the wrong crowd. Maybe he just said it because he wanted Gretchen back. You know, Toby wasn't much to look at, he smelled and everything, but inside he was a right guy. Not easy to do what he did, dry out, get a job, go back after your kid."

"Remind me to tip you more next I'm inside."

"Will do." Wally looks down the street, sees the sidewalk emptying into The Farm, goes back to sucking his teeth. "Well, I'm late. Bastards'll be bawlin' for beer and my dogs barkin' already."

"Even on a Sunday."

Wally nodded.

X

Telling Wally about Toby is as good as having it blasted over The Farm's PA system. Soon anyone who cares will know. Meg should be back at the hotel. It's Sunday and traffic is semi-thick, streetcars swishing their doors closed then clacking deep into the Beaches. Two young women stride by like they've some place to go. An old man strolls with his face up to the sun.

✦ ✦ ✦

It was quiet Friday night, I remember, when we left The Farm. I scanned the shadows for signs of Neville and Cecil.

"Well I'm bushed," Meg said like she and Cecil hadn't been tongue-swabbing each other's tonsils moments earlier.

My watch said near midnight. In town one night and she'd had me in two fights. A win and a draw. Blood still thumped in my ears. Can't say I didn't enjoy it, but I was still trying to figure out what it meant. Was she using other men to tease me, test me, or using me as safety while she played with other men? A long pull on the flask. Meg didn't want any.

"You were quick off the mark," she said, finally.

"Cecil's younger and faster than me. Only thing I had going was surprise."

"Why'd you stop?" Little trill of excitement in her voice.

Liz had hated the idea of me fighting, but you can't always avoid it on the job. Use the authority of the uniform and in your voice to take charge early in any situation, but it didn't always work.

80

"Neville. That and Cecil brought out a blade when I swung. If Neville hadn't said something, you might be stitching my boxers back together right now."

"Oh, I don't sew," she said.

Liz used to complain I brought cop techniques home. Said I never talked, just barked. I don't say she was wrong, but I didn't see it that way. Whatever I have going with Meg, I haven't noticed her jump when I speak. Another pull on the flask.

"A walk then. I need the air."

We went east, past a block of empty new storefront windows powdered with drywall dust. Some have signs promising new businesses about to open. Windows across the street are vacant or boarded.

"I didn't see a knife."

"An exacto-blade. A packing knife," I said. "You weren't meant to see it. I was."

Technically the Beaches is a strip of sand and park along the shore of Lake Ontario. The neighbourhood is a mix of worker's cottages and bigger homes anchored by a strip of shops on Queen St. for residents and day-tourists who escape the summer heat for the price of a streetcar ticket. The old Woodbine racetrack used to sit immediately west of the Beaches, catching downtown traffic before it reached the snow-cones, under-cooked hot dogs and the lake's other chilly charms.

Now the snow-cones have lost out to iced cappuccinos. No shift-labourer on the straight and narrow could carry a mortgage here today. Big houses are split into swank condos, but still the district is too small to contain a real-estate agent's imagination. The old track has been knocked down for condominium towers and wedged-in semis. A sign christens the place "Olde Woodbine Estates." Fake gingerbread has spread across the old back fields and parking lots like some white, eaves-eating fungus. Put driveways up the side instead of an alley round back, this could be any suburb in North America.

We turned in to the survey of homes. The corner sales office and model homes were closed. Blocks of brick-veneered houses, windows filled with the yellow light of early buyers snuggled into their recent big purchase.

"Neville and Cecil and me were never close," I explained. "Just light entertainment I met at The Farm. But we never fought before either."

"Don't blame me. I just tried to fit in."

"Cecil might say the same thing."

"He kissed me. I was as surprised as you were."

"Looked to me you enjoyed it."

"Well we were having fun, and I did for the moment." She stopped walking and pulled me round to face her. "Look at me John. Don't confuse me with your so-called friends. They pulled the knife. I'm here with you. But don't expect me to change who I am because you can't hold your liquor."

"That what you think it was?" I lifted the flask again, thinking, don't try changing me, either.

She smiled. "You were rather dashing, in your way."

We toasted *dashing* with the flask from Meg's purse. Mine was drained. Another splash because the chill was in off the lake. Meg gathered her jacket to her throat, but we walked on until the houses were empty shells.

"Let's window shop," Meg said, pulling me up a gravel strip. The house was shelled, the inside rough-framed. "Half bath," she said, looking right, into the small room just inside the entrance.

"Living room," I added, looking into the larger room on the left. "Dining room at the back beyond."

"Kitchen straight ahead," Meg turned and led upstairs, running her hand along the unpainted wall where a handrail would soon be installed.

On the second floor, bare wood studs divided the area into three large rooms and smaller spaces for closets and two pissers. In new homes, kids need never learn their parents even shit, let alone that it smells.

Meg started to leave the largest bedroom, but I put my arms around her waist. "Pretty soon some nice young couple will begin banging the headboard here once a week," I said. "Spawn another generation of misfits. Jobs for cops, social workers and bad guitarists."

It earned me a grin. "Only once a week? Why once a week?"

"Too tired from paying off the mortgage for anything more. Suppose we might break the joint in for them?"

Something about the promise of wet heat in a woman on a cool night. I pulled her close, the top of her head just under my nose. Her hair was different at the scalp, whiter and darker.

"What? Here?" she asked, staring at the dusty floor.

I looked down and imagined her jeans and panties on the floor. I saw her bare-assed on a cross-brace between the studs, me doing the mambo-jambo between her knees, my shorts at my ankles. It wouldn't sound nearly this romantic if I had to put it into words for her. Giggles downstairs.

She gave me a peck. "Bloody cold," she said, pulling the collar up on her windbreaker. More giggles. A thump. "I think there's someone down there," she said, facing the stairwell.

Meg wanted to go, but now she listened, the couple downstairs making their own heat. I moved my hands up under her pink windbreaker. She pushed them away.

"They'll hear us," she said.

"So?"

She led me back down, stopped to peek at the bodies coiled in the dust of the dining room floor. I admired their lean, uncomplicated youth, the statements of their dyed, short, spiked hair in the moonlight, their unrestrained endurance.

"Have a good night," I said, and went out to the sidewalk.

✦ ✦ ✦

We walked some more, finishing the flask from Meg's purse. I remember passing the Italian café close to the hotel.

"Guys at The Farm say this is a mob hangout," I told Meg. It's never seemed busy enough to me to be called a hangout, but who knows? Maybe it's a small mob, sort of a mobette.

We must have gone inside. We had the cement-block building to ourselves, except for the counter guy who turned out also to be waiter, chef and busboy. I ordered a slice and a beer. The slice had been under the heat lamp too long. The beer was cold. Meg had pasta with oil and spinach and feta cheese and I think sun-dried tomatoes. Greek spaghetti, I called it, and probably the grease-spotted menu did too, except in Italian.

A white Buick entered the parking lot. A big guy came through the door with an empty insulated delivery bag. How can it pay to deliver pizza in a fucking gas-sucking Buick? Meg flashed the big guy her pearlies. He ignored her, said a few words to the waiter/chef/busboy who'd come out to see who came in. They both went back to the kitchen.

Everything depends, I suppose, on what goes into the bag with the pizza. There's a lot of things could fit easy in those flat square boxes: condoms, a dime bag, a few grams of white powder. Hell, a sawed-off Remington 11R 12-gauge Riot Gun would fit if you broke it down. Takeout weaponry delivered under the cover of a hot meal. Good when The Family goes to the mattresses. Careful selecting the toppings. Don't want a slice of mushroom or a loose bit of anchovy gumming up the firing pin during a shootout.

We took cappuccinos back to the hotel. It was raining, a steady drizzle that sent light streaking down the dark pavements. City smell washed from the air. Empty sidewalks. I imagined people chased by the rain into sharp, roadside shadows when the drizzle began. The liquor store was closed, the usual line of taxicabs outside gone. The other side of Queen Street was brilliantly deserted. No one entered or left the multiplex theatre. No one rushed to lay down a last-minute bet at The Farm. A bus wheezed to a stop outside the Java Hut, but only the driver got off, for a whiz and a refill.

Maybe this was another time, because I remember holding Meg briefly in the hotel parking lot, but I didn't have the cardboard cappuccino in my hand anymore. Maybe we finished them, tossed them into the street. Or maybe I've just imagined this bit. It's Friday, or the small hours of Saturday morning. We've been to The Onion, to The Farm, and finally the new housing development, before landing here. If there were murmurs or cries silenced in the hotel parking lot, Meg and I didn't hear them. Inside, the desk clerk had his back to the lobby when we entered. A long hallway of closed doors from the elevator to our room, and the Heaven Heather brought from home.

XI

Meg is dressed and waiting in the room when I get back from talking to Wally. She puts down her new book. Doesn't look like she's gotten far with it.

"Where'd you go?" I ask.

"Walked around. You were sleeping. I wasn't sleeping so I went out. You weren't here when I got back."

I tell her about meeting Wally, what he had to say. She's excited by it. "I put Friday night together too," I tell her.

"But you started without me," she pouts.

"Started what?"

A colour brochure fallen down behind the TV says the hotel offers five channels of pay porno. The shiny card looks older than the flesh in the flicks on offer. It also has directions to the preview channel.

"What do you want to do now?" she says.

"Catch the bus home, I guess. Steam's kind of gone out of this weekend, don't you think?"

She comes up behind me, her hands slipping through my arms like snakes, linking across my stomach. "I think there's still some things left undone."

"What's on your mind?"

"I'd like to see how you investigate, find out things about people."

"I told you before. You ask and people tell you what happened. Their version anyway. There's nothing magic or exciting about it."

I flick the remote. There's a preview of the porno channel way up the dial. It doesn't show much, mostly moaning. *Nookie Night in*

Canada, *The Bushwackers*, *An Oral History of Toronto*, and finally *What's Up Doctor Ruth*.

She teases. "We might become a famous detective couple. Like *Hart to Hart*."

Liz used to watch that. "The Harts were rich. Made their butler do all the heavy lifting."

"Okay, not *Hart to Hart*. There must be other couples who've turned a buck doing investigations."

I turn into her embrace. "Why? You need a job?"

"Not me. I'm in it for kicks. Don't you want to find out what happened to your friend?"

"First, there are no kicks. Second, you made the point Friday night that guys at The Farm aren't actually friends. More like acquaintances. As for Toby, he delivered diapers: forty hours a week in a van full of piss-soaked rags. Killing him was practically a public service. If he wasn't murdered, he'd probably die of a brain tumour or full-body diaper rash. Tell you the truth, I miss my chevy more."

"Well then we'll clear your name with that detective," she says.

We sit on the edge of the bed. The clinch holds. "My name's as clear with him as it's likely to get. Nothing to be gained in a pissing contest with that son of a bitch."

"The sooner the case is solved, the sooner you get the chevy back." A peck on my left cheek.

She's found a weak spot. "I'm not sure it's worth having back. It's sure taken a beating since I met you."

"You blame me?" A peck on my right cheek.

"I'm just saying. It's going to need someone to pop the panels back out."

"You should drive it as it is." A peck on my lips. "It's so you."

The porno preview loops through a couple times while I consider what's better: the hockey at twelve bucks, the porno four-pack at just under twenty bucks, or Meg on the bed.

She must read minds. "I can do more for you than hotel pornography. How men can watch a two-hour show about something that's over so quick is beyond me."

"We watch them in spurts," I tell her and switch off the remote. "What became of that little red nightie I bought yesterday? That was yesterday, wasn't it?"

"Are you afraid of Topcoat? Did he put his finger up your ass last night like Crouch said they do?" Her hand moves down my back.

"It gets done, believe me."

"Oh I do. I think somebody's put a stick up there already."

"You really want to do this?"

She plants a longer kiss on my lips, but she could still be my sister. "I do, yes. It'll be fun." Her arms fall from my body. "What do you want me to do?"

"Put on the red nightie." I think I made that clear.

"Be serious now."

"I am serious. Get undressed. Forget the nightie."

"But you're filthy. You haven't washed or shaved since we got here."

I stand, pour from the bottle of Heaven Heather into one of the tumblers on top of the dresser, drain half. Refill. Sniff under my arms. She has a point.

"I'll take a shower."

"I'll meet you..."

"No. You stay. I want you here when I get out. Tell me more about Saturday, you want something to do."

"You want to remember," Meg says, "start with the last thing you remember and tell..."

"No. You want me to remember Saturday. I remember buying the red nightie. Beyond that, I couldn't care less. But you want me to investigate Toby's murder, make like a pigeon and coo."

"That's all you remember? The red nightie?"

"I remember Toby found his kid, but I don't know how I know that."

✦ ✦ ✦

"Saturday we went to The Farm twice," Meg says. "Toby was there both times. He had the kid with him in the afternoon. Her name was Gretchen."

I remember. She was cute. Dyed, stamped, stapled and booted, all the street accessories but on reasonably scrubbed flesh. "This place is so lame," she had said, like we didn't already know.

Toby didn't like the way she spoke. "What? All kinds of people here. Mr. Swan's a detective, you know, and the lady he's with, what is it you do miss?" he asked.

"Whatever I need to," Meg answered.

"Meg, Toby, Toby, Meg," I said. "And this is the missing Gretchen happily discovered, I'm guessing."

Toby continued. "The people come here do all sorts of things, and they'll talk to you, no puttin' on the fancy airs." He nodded across the room to where two men in dark blue golf shirts swept the floor and cleared tables. "Enviro-mentalists, here. All sorts."

"Wearing a white mask while you empty ashtrays does not make you an environmentalist," Gretchen said. "I'm going to tell mother. I shouldn't even be inside a room where people smoke cigarettes."

"Who would you rather have smoke them?" Meg asked.

"Mother is Val," I tell Meg, having a hard time in the tiny hotel bathroom getting my arms out of my sleeves. "A woman Wally just told me didn't give a shit one way or the other about Gretchen."

I'd have my shirt off if I could turn diagonally, but it's up over my head. I can't see. My elbow's jammed between the window frame and the shower rod. Should have got undressed in the bedroom.

"We talked to Gretchen for a while," Meg says to me now.

Toby blew smoke out his nose, put his butt in our tray and moved it to the side away from his daughter. "I gotta stay to the fourth in Hialieah Park," he said. To us: "A sure thing. I can share it with you too." To Gretchen: "Then we'll do whatever you want, okay?"

Gretchen pinched her lips and squinted.

My pants and shorts around my ankles on the bathroom floor. I've torn the armpit out of my shirt. My socks are the problem. I can sit on the can, but I don't think there's room between it and the sink for me to bend over and reach my feet. Another thing, I'm bigger than the tub is wide. The shower curtain will be like a big muumuu, but it isn't going to keep water in.

"We had some drinks," Meg says from the bedroom.

Wally grunted up to the side of our table.

"Sleeman's Ale," Gretchen said, "and make it a clean glass."

Wally's eyes got wetter at the sorry state of youth in his world.

"Bring her another Coke, Wally. 'N'other ice-tea for me, okay? You want some chips baby?"

Gretchen didn't answer.

"You two just carry on." Wally said. "Don't mind us."

I shook my head, already tired of Toby's domestic life. Meg went into the larger room to figure out how the betting machines worked. She passed four empty machines to watch three young guys, baseball caps shading where they'd been, manipulate a betting box like it was a pinball game.

"Some nice boys showed me how to use the betting machines," she says from the bedroom.

I'm waiting for the water to warm. My clothes are on the toilet tank. Hell with the socks.

The boys looked too young to be legal, but maybe that's me. Anybody wears their cap backwards has to be under fifteen, I figure. I strolled to the snack booth on the far side. It had burgers, tacos and hot dogs, pop, chips and popcorn. All the major food groups. We could have eaten there if I'd wanted to eat alone. I asked for tea. Took five minutes for them to find the bags, but tea doesn't sludge in the bottom of the cup the way their coffee does.

"You talked to some man who looked like a mechanic," Meg says.

Hard to hear over the water splash. I ask her to repeat.

Malcolm, face already shadowed in dark stubble, rested his elbow on a counter by the door. He looked like a mechanic because he is. Mid-afternoon, he was stealing time from work. He'd taken off his coveralls, but he hadn't scrubbed his nails and grease glinted in his thinning jelly roll. So he still had work to do back at the garage.

"Had my tubes cut this morning," he said. For the moment I thought he was installing new equipment in the service bays, but he set me straight. "Snip snip." Scissor motions with his nicotine fingers. "Wife said it was time so I went and had 'em done. What I told her anyway, case she asks. Thought I'd come down here, kill the time. Don't tell her you seen me. Anything good?"

"Don't know. Haven't bought a form yet."

"I could have got you that." This was Wally passing. He meant the tea. He was right. He could have. He'd have charged me two bucks, taken twice as long and wanted a tip. It's only since then that I learned he deserved it.

I watched Meg at the betting machines, lightly touching young shoulders and hands as the boys showed her which buttons did what when she pressed them to enter her choices.

"How's the old chevy running?" Malcolm asked. He always does.

"Purrs like a fat, contented cat."

"Bring it by, you ever plan to get rid of it. It's a classic."

"Classic what?"

"I'm not kiddin'. You ever decide to sell, I'll get you ten times what you'd get from a dealer. No shit. Split it fifty-fifty."

"Super. Five times nothing," I said. "Won't be worth anything when I'm done with it."

"You tow her in, I'll get her running. Flip the pink no time. Longer you wait, more she's worth. I'm not kidding, don't forget me now."

"I'll put you on my speed dial," I said.

The shower shifts from almost warm to bitter cold. There's no room to run. "Did you wi—"

"What?"

It comes back to almost warm again. "The betting machine. You figure out how to use it?"

"We bet ten dollars, just to see what would happen."

Her ten. I watched her lean over to pick a horse from their racing form, her breasts grazing lean, young forearms. She took plastic from her purse, swiped it through the machine and the boys punched in their pick. She cheered the horse with them under the TV screens, just like she had with Cecil. She squealed with them when they won. She took their slip to the windows down front to get paid and divided the money, giving each boy a kiss on the cheek. Then she came back my way.

"Did you win?" I shout again.

"They helped me learn the machine, so I said I'd let them have the winnings. It only cost me ten dollars that way. You want to learn new technology, ask the young, I always say. Cheaper than a college course."

"Don't think they have a college course on betting at the race track."

"They do, actually. I was going to take one once, but..."

By the time she returned I was sitting with Crouch, who'd rolled up to the end of a bench facing the betting windows outside the smokers' lounge. "What you doing out here?" Though I already knew the answer.

"Hiding from Toby and that kid. Jesus, ain't she a treat."

"It's a phase. This place can't be much of a thrill for her."

"You got kids, Swanee?"

"A daughter, up in Ottawa last we spoke. Nearly old as you." Crouch had majored in psychology at several universities. Made a career of it, thanks to student loans. Last trip he'd told me he was trying correspondence. By telepathy, most like.

"Where you staying?" he asked.

"Hotel across the road."

"Woman like that," he nodded as Meg approached, "thought you'd be at the Coxwell Inn."

"There is no Coxwell Inn, Crouch. You need a new joke." I contemplated my tea.

"No offense." He burrowed into the racing form, then tried again. "Malcolm tell you about his vasectomy?"

"Yep."

"Wife put him up to it. They don't have kids, but she thinks he's been catting around. Thinks this will put an end to it. I think she's confused."

"When do you talk to Malcolm's wife?" I asked. A close-lipped smile grew on his face.

"You're full of shit," I said.

Suddenly there's Toby's voice bursting from the smokers' lounge. "Okay we'll sit out here where there's no smoking. Hey Crouch, Swanee."

"We talked to Crouch," Meg says, "and Toby and Gretchen again."

There's not enough room to wash everything in this shower, but I get most of it before dropping the soap. I turn the water off, watch the last bit twist over the rust ring round the drain then disappear.

"Crouch wasn't very nice to Toby," Meg says.

"Crouch isn't very nice to anybody," I answer.

"Thought you said last night you had work today," Crouch said. It didn't discourage Toby. He sat next to me while Gretchen shifted her weight in the aisle behind Crouch. She'd decided there was still mileage left on her frown.

"Well, I only just found Gretchen this morning so I phoned in sick. More time for us to be together, eh Gretch? Make up for last night?" He brought wet lips close to my ear. There's the diaper truck smell. "Only Saturday anyways. Half day."

Over by the counter where he could waylay Wally or anyone else who'd listen to his ballroom fables, Malcolm eyeballed a woman with thin, grim lips. Her skirt was short, showing a lot of black stocking. She'd given the ballcap boys the once-over, moved in after Meg was done, but Meg had left them thinking they could do better. They giggled. Hard to split one blowjob three ways. Black Stockings caught Malcolm's stare, zeroed in like she knew what she was doing. I suppose Malcolm did too.

"Nothing much was happening," Meg says as I stumble out of the bathroom. The shower curtain's come with me. "So we left."

I stood, waited for Crouch to roll back, let me out.

"Gonna finish that tea?" he asked.

XII

Meg is still fully dressed. She doesn't move to get into the red nightie as I towel off.

"I could murder a plate of chops," she says. "Let's go to The Onion. I know you like it there." Like it's a favour. Because I like it there. A sacrifice she's willing to make.

"Suddenly The Onion is okay by you. Last night you wouldn't go near the place. This morning you didn't want to talk about it."

"John, The Onion's not much to talk about, but it has good food. Besides, it was you didn't want to go there last night."

"Don't think so."

"Yes it was."

I remember sitting in that Beaches pub, after the sex boutique, Meg still shopping while I waited.

"Smithwicks on tap?" I asked the bartender.

"Pint?"

I nodded. "No, wait. How about a single malt?"

"I've got something you'll like."

He poured gold into a glass, water sparkling on the side. I mixed, swirled, sniffed, sipped and smiled.

"An '81 Dalwhinnie," he said. "Taste the highland peat?"

"Why? He fall into the vat?"

Closest I've ever been to a bog in Scotland was watching Liz spread sphagnum around the marigolds. But this was a joint to put on the dog. No sports bar, the lone screen on the wall behind the counter was tuned to a news channel: weather, traffic, financial reports sharing space with a yokel promising disaster in mock surprise. I opened the paper I'd bought with Meg in the bookstore.

I was reading how the 'Spos and the Habs are destined to leave Montreal when a familiar voice murmured just inside the doorway. It was Neville, asking for a table. He didn't see me. Man next to him, shiny suit, dark hair greying at the temples, tucked a pair of sunglasses into his breast pocket, gave his ear to Neville's chatter. They followed the hostess to a booth at the back. They took menus. They ordered pints. Neville looked too busy to appreciate me shouting hello and I sure as shit didn't want any company, other than Meg's. Neville asked for the table but the hostess didn't know him from street shine. She spoke to his accessory instead, "Right this way Mr. Cartwright."

I remember wondering then if Cecil knew he had competition for Neville's attentions, but hearing the Cartwright name again today from Wally, I think it might be something else entirely.

"I'd just ordered a second drink when you took the stool next to me," I tell Meg. "You opened a brown paper bag, showed me fresh underwear and toothpaste, essential provisions for the rest of the weekend. I'd have left right then, but not for The Onion."

"You did say let's go somewhere else."

"Right, and I put twenty on the counter for the barman. He walked down, said it was $34.70 with tax. I laid out another twenty and said a prayer for the price of beer at The Farm. Tell the truth, I felt beat up. And when it was all done, I still knew what I wanted, but you decided where we went next."

"You didn't like it?" Meg asks.

She'd found a place that had escargot on the menu. I ordered shrimp cocktail and bubbly because I've always had a weakness since watching the Blues Brothers chow down at Chez Paul in Chi-town. I also tried a bite from a dessert Meg said was too decadent to eat alone. We ordered coffee, then more wine, sweeter than before. I got my own helping of dessert, to show I knew a thing or two about decadence. Meg paid.

"I'm not complaining," I say. "I'm just asking, when do we get to that red nightie?" Saturday afternoon is now complete in my memory.

"These things are better with anticipation, don't you think?"

"I'm on the downside of anticipation Meg. I'm on the upside of getting pissed off."

"Well really John, what type of girl do you take me for?"

She's struck a Sue-Anne pose, one that needs countering. I drop my towel, sit naked and ready in the room's one chair, wedged between the dresser and bathroom door. "I don't take you for a girl. I take you for a woman. The type of woman who invites herself on a weekend sally at the Beaches Hotel with a man she's recently met. Don't get me wrong. I like that kind of woman. I didn't object because—"

"You didn't object because you thought you'd get laid. You thought I'd be your hotel whore."

These are the moments when it's good to smoke. The little social ritual of lighting up provides a brief pause, a chance to reflect. "I'm attracted to you. The attraction is sexual. And something more, maybe. I liked the idea of having you with me. Better than being here on my own. That's getting tired. I wanted to see where this feeling led, whether it would stand up, but now I don't know. You offer your-self to everyone but me. I don't get it. Really. I want to, but I don't."

She squints, scratches polish from the nail of the third finger on her left hand until. "I told you I was a model," she starts.

"And I said bully for you."

"Model is the polite word."

I draw a deep breath, pick up my towel, let it rest on my lap.

"I was a teen when I went to Milan. They go younger now, fif-teen, fourteen. I started the usual way, stage mom stuff, modelling school, beauty pageants, dance lessons from the time I could walk. I was good at it. I learned poise from the dancing. I learned makeup. I learned clothes. I learned what the camera wanted."

"You're a beautiful woman, Meg."

She rummages her purse, comes up with a butt and lighter. "That's sweet dear, but it's not what the modelling business is about. Surprised?"

A trick question. "Don't know enough about it to be surprised."

"There was a contest," she continues, "run by a big New York agency. They do this every year across North America. I didn't win, but they sent me to Italy anyway. I'd learn more there in a week than in a lifetime at home. I'd meet important, international designers, big-name photographers. I'd stay in a chaperoned dormitory near the agency's Italian office. If I worked hard, there'd be contracts for me after I got back. You should have seen how mother pushed me out the door. 'Here's ten dollars from your uncle Freddy.'"

"Ten bucks?"

"It was worth more then, and he wasn't really my uncle so he thought he was really doing something. He smiled so big his fillings showed. Mother couldn't handle the competition, so she walked me onto the plane.

"The chaperones were pretty Italian boys with five o'clock shadows. They travelled to the big fashion shows, rode around in Porsches and limousines though the agency didn't pay them enough for a second-hand scooter. And they always had something to help their girls get over homesickness, to keep them 'up.' Everybody should be 'up' all the time: mornings when a black-shirt in garters cracked her riding crop to keep our backs straight and chins up; afternoons when the paunchy executives came down from the studios to watch us try on their clothes; nights when the chaperones took us to nightclubs and accepted money from businessmen who wanted to sit with us."

"These 'chaperones,' they sound like pimps."

"You know Swanee, you should have been a cop. There was a party every night, booze, shit, and getting fucked by old Italians in thousand dollar suits who paid for the booze and shit. Or there was going home. I phoned my mother, told her I wanted to leave. She said 'Stick it out dear, it'll be worthwhile. Your uncle Freddy's cheering for you.' Getting away from her was probably the only worthwhile thing about Milan. So I learned to get along. I learned what a camera likes, understand?"

There's something about social history that doesn't support a hard-on. No point in the towel. I squeeze beside the bed for my gym bag, change of underwear. Stucco from the wall scratches my naked thigh. "Not exactly."

"The camera doesn't like anything. It's just a camera. It's a man behind the camera has things he likes, doesn't like. What he likes is more. Men always want more. Everyone knows the model is a tease. Soon as 'more' is delivered, or it's clear that 'more' is not going to be delivered, the tease is finished. That's the most important thing a model can learn.

"My chaperone was Carlo. Late twenties with bad teeth. Always rubbing his crotch and calling it 'petting the stallion.' I learned I didn't need him. How much talent does it take to meet men in bars? Milan was full of men with wives who didn't understand them. Some were even handsome, successful and polite, with no smell from the fashion business. It didn't take long to find one who met my specifications."

"Which were?"

"Clean, generous and unwilling to share with Carlo or his clients. Of course Carlo made a fuss. The agreement mother signed made the agency my legal guardian while I was in Italy. As chaperone Carlo could call the police if I tried to leave. He was already fucking most of the models in his charge in return for the drugs and favours he provided. He couldn't afford the example of one that got away. He threatened to put me on a plane home. Stupid bastard. A week earlier I might have fucked him for that ticket alone. Now I had Paulo.

"Paulo was willing to pay Carlo a reasonable buy out, that was just business in Milan. But Carlo wouldn't let go until I 'kissed the stallion.' If I had to I'd have given him a letter of recommendation, but I wasn't going to write it with my tongue. He became enraged, tore at his pants. 'You go nowhere till you've had this.' The way he held onto it, you'd think it was the fucking Tower of Pisa. I pretended to melt, aimed and performed what I considered an acceptable jeté, deflating him with the well-aimed four-inch heel on my Rossari sandal."

"Huh?" I'm a bit mystified.

"I kicked him in the groin, ran downstairs to the agency office, broke in and called Paulo, who brought two cars. One to dispose of Carlo, and the limousine to carry me to an apartment Paulo owned in Genoa. I spent two years in Italy. I travelled. I visited museums and art galleries. I monitored courses at the American University. And I entertained Paulo. He was just one man and I could tease him with the thrill of a postponed reward. Eventually, of course, even his interest flagged. I told him I missed my family in Canada and introduced him to a model from Australia. Paulo and I flew to Montreal together. He helped me find an apartment, introduced me to some banker friends he knew and after a week, he went back to Milan."

It's quiet enough now to hear the streetcar pass outside. She's waiting. I'm supposed to say something. "So, I should be patient?"

"Remember I said I never fucked any man if it wasn't my choice? That's true, but also, I've never fucked anyone I loved either."

I draw wind. I shake my head.

"And I think I might love you John."

I admit, I'm confused.

"I've been engaged, shit I've lost count. I was married, long enough to understand parenthood was never part of the package. Well to hell with that, I'd make a worse mother than my own and I'm past that anyway. So after Ham, it's back to fundraising."

"Didn't you get Ham's estate?"

"We rented the apartment we lived in. He got the cottage in his divorce, but I've received notice his ex is suing to get that back. It isn't winterized so I can't live in it more than four months a year anyway, and she got an injunction so I can't sell it."

"There's the insurance."

Meg laughs. "Yes, there's that, but it's not so much as Jim Crandall would lead you to believe. And here's the part you'll appreciate most. Janet's lawsuit over the cottage doesn't have much merit. My lawyer says she would probably lose, but that could take years. Janet doesn't mind because her son, Ham's son too, is her lawyer, so it doesn't cost her much. But the defense will chew through all the insurance money and you know I'm just waiting for Janet to file a suit to take that from me too. So I'm back to fundraising, only it's coming to an end. I'm not a kid any more. I'm fed up with it anyway. It was only ever a tax-deductible fuck, a way to skim a living from money the rich give to their self-serving charities: doctors seeding drives for new hospital wings; lawyers spawning make-work legislation; business associations lobbying to have their taxes cut. Everybody swelling political coffers and me flirting like hell to be the bigger bang for their bucks. Except I'm already older than my competition. Pretty soon they won't have a use for me."

"You want to pool resources, your insurance and my pension?" I ask. "Together we could do more than scratch along." I don't mind that.

"My best shot might be to spend the insurance quick and rent out the cottage to the Hell's Angels."

I sit up straight. "I've always aspired to be better company than the Hell's."

"You've been fun. I like fun, but I need it on my terms now. Like the fundraising circuit, it's just a club, understand? The old-school wanking circle, bum-pat on the playing field, flicking towels in the locker room. A cocksucking club, no getting in without one or

strapping one on. The years I spent flattering those pompous bastards, and they think they're done with me? Well I'm not finished
with them. I want my retirement benefits. I've paid attention over
the years. They all think they're so smart, so competent, but they
screw up like everybody else. Back home, I know where and how they
do their screwing up. I'd like to fuck them over for a change, just for
fun and whatever loose cash falls out, but I need help."

"So, what? I'm your strap-on?"

"Something like that. I can't do this alone. I'm not stupid. Maybe
it's the same everywhere, but one thing I know for certain, in our
town women get stuffed into car trunks or put out on curbs in
garbage bags for doing what I've got in mind. I need a partner who
knows how to pick a fight and isn't afraid to stick it."

There are a dozen reasons to do what she wants. None of them
good, except like Sue-Anne Robinson said on the night she introduced me to Meg, I'm hanging around, sucking on a bottle of Heaven
Heather, waiting for nothing. And I'm sick of doing it alone.

"Doesn't sound like *Hart to Hart*."

"Like you said, they were rich already."

I pinch a cigarette from Meg's deck where she's left it on the bed.
"Still, no sex, huh?"

She leans forward, lets me see the full weight of her breasts
against the fabric of her sweater. "I didn't say that. I said it's better if
you anticipate it."

"So why should we hang around here?"

"There's money here. I could smell it Friday when we arrived.
Plus, you seem to know the locals the way I know the crowd back
home. Or at least you can find out about them. Didn't Wally tell you
that Toby, who we know is suing for full custody of Gretchen,
works for Neville? And both this Cartwright and O'Keefe smell
overripe to me."

"Seriously though, this isn't some TV show, with car chases and
'takedowns.'"

"They have the real police on TV now, John."

"Hell they do. They have hot-dogs setting up phony busts to
make themselves look good on camera. They don't show what comes
before, hours sitting out in the cold pissing into paper cups while the
bad guys talk on the telephone laughing at you."

Her face goes white. "Really? You mean Hollywood doesn't tell the truth? Next thing you'll say there's no Batman or Robin. No Gotham full of innocent victims and everyone in crap up to their necks. Or maybe everyone is up to their necks and you don't see the possibilities."

"First thing," I say, "is to double check what we've heard from Wally, and find out what we can about Gretchen, who seems to be the other link between Neville and Cartwright and O'Keefe."

"Who's O'Keefe again?"

"Gretchen's grandfather. Lives in Ancaster. Ever come across him in your fundraising?"

"Not that I recall. I don't quite see—"

"Where did Toby get the money to go up against Cartwright and O'Keefe's deep pockets in custody court? And why now, when the kid's nearly a legal adult? You've met him. Did Toby strike you as father material on Saturday? But Toby works for Neville and yesterday I saw Neville working some kind of relationship with Cartwright."

"Are Cartwright and O'Keefe linked? I mean, necessarily? Couldn't Cartwright be working with Neville on his own?"

"Well, they're father and son-in-law, and they're both linked to the Olde Woodbine Estates development, but you're right. We don't know if there's anything more for sure. We only know enough to investigate further."

"But we do know Neville's into other things."

"If we believe Wally," I say, and turn over my hand. "There might be some angle we can make pay. We have to poke into it. We're here anyway." It's what she wants and it's better than sitting home alone. "Won't have the chevy back for a few days at least. Besides, you know what Topcoat told me before he let me go."

Her lips come up on one side.

"Don't leave town," we say together.

Part 3

XIII

"Where we going?" Meg pulls the collars of her jacket close.

"Quick check in The Farm. See if there's anyone else can tell us more about Toby."

But the only familiar face belongs to Ivan. I remember his answer when I told him about Toby: "Da." Just that, like it was to be expected.

Ivan doesn't smoke, at least he doesn't sit in the smoking lounge with the rest of us. Don't recall exactly when we first met. I've been nodding hello for years, when he'd approach our table to talk with Neville. It's late afternoon, and he's pushing buttons on an arcade machine in the big room. After a bit the lights stop flashing and the machine makes a sound like a jet engine winding down. Ivan slaps it on the side.

"When I spoke to you this afternoon, you didn't seem surprised that Toby had been killed," I say.

He takes the toothpick from his mouth. "Da, I see him yesterday with that girl, same as everybody. Is trouble you want, fucking young girls from the street is how you get."

"That was his dau..." a quick toe-tap to Meg's ankle shuts her up. "Have you seen the kid before?" she asks instead.

The dark eyes become hooded. "Why I should tell you?"

"Because if you do my friend here will give you ten bucks for the next sure thing on the race card," I say.

The dark look becomes a squint. "Why you want to know?"

I shake my head. "One or the other. Ten bucks or trade information, take your pick."

The look doesn't change, but a hand comes out. Meg digs into her purse.

"I see her plenty, but not here. I think, she is too young for old men who bet horses. But I think too she is too old for the boys," he shrugs, dipping his head. "They are cleaning car windows and hanging around. They are with her when I see her other times."

"Where? Where would I find her?"

"That is worth more than ten dollars, no?"

Meg is still digging in her purse. "Not yet."

"She is around here many places. Little India I see her and sometimes over in the Kew Park. Sometimes down on the beach. But that is more summertime. I see them lately going into where is the new houses, now it gets colder at night."

"Them? She's running with a gang?"

"I tell you already the boys who are making change cleaning car windows when they stop for the lights. Over there, Coxwell," pointing to the south, where Coxwell meets Lakeshore.

"Cops put an end to that."

He brings his hands together, palms up, and the shrug again. "Yes, is a shame boys cannot earn money, but I tell you it is the same ones she is still being with."

"Give him twenty," I tell Meg.

"Don't see why I'm the one has to pay him."

"You're the one thought it would be fun." That and I'm running low. Back to Ivan: "You see her a lot?"

He smiles. "I like this area. Is nice, cheap to live. Always something is happening." He taps the side of his head, close to his left eye. "And is always good to pay attention."

"What do you mean? Someone else interested in the girl or Toby?"

He shakes his head. "That is something, who wants to know what, that is worth hundreds of dollars."

I look at Meg.

"No. No way. I'm not giving him a hundred dollars."

"Could save us plenty of time."

"Time is what we've plenty of," she says.

I show Ivan how I can shrug too. Good. We're all fatalists. Meg and I go outside, head east toward the new housing survey that reaches around behind The Farm.

106

"We can't just go handing out hundreds of dollars for every little tidbit of information. I'll be broke in no time."

"How it's done. Not always with money of course. Cops have authority to trade on. They can roust a guy like Ivan, trade information for letting him go."

"What's Ivan done that would get him arrested?"

"I don't know. Anything. Look hard enough, there's always something."

"So what are we doing here?"

"Friday, the two kids screwing downstairs in the new house we toured? I couldn't say for sure, but I thought the girl looked a bit like Gretchen."

"It was so dark, John."

We turn the corner into Olde Woodbine Estates. Meg huddles against the wind coming in from the lake.

"Yeah, but she was on top. And Ivan just said this was one of the places he'd seen her hanging around."

"She won't still be here will she?"

"You heard him. They use these houses now the weather's started to turn. Better than a bus shelter or condemned industrial site. Plenty of construction rubbish around to burn for heat. If she's not here, maybe one of her friends. But you're probably wondering why she'd stay here when she's got a nice home in the suburbs."

"Nope. Makes perfect sense to me."

"Too bad, because that's one of the things we should find out."

The survey is bigger than it looked on Friday. Now it's big as a haystack. But the kids won't be in one of the sold and occupied houses. That narrows it down to maybe a dozen units. I march up the concrete paving slabs to the front door of the first vacant house.

The first house is empty. So are the next two. We've been at it about an hour now. The sky has started to darken when a white cruiser with red and blue stripes down the side and yellow flashers rolling on the roof waits for us at the foot of another drive. The siren whoops and a man gets out: blue shirt with epaulets, midnight blue polyester pants, leather pouches and a silver key chain on his belt. We crunch down the gravel to the passenger side of the prowler. He has short, black hair and the crests on his shoulders and the sides of his car are only similar to Metro cops'. His left hand holds a small, black, two-way radio. He looks about twenty-plus, and eager to hold something more authoritative than a walkie-talkie.

"This is private property. The sales office is closed, except by appointment," he says.

"Thanks officer. I'm looking for the gang of kids who kip in the vacant units here."

"What?"

"Kip. Sleep. Make camp."

He shakes his head slowly. "Nope. No sir. Not here. These streets get a patrol car every hour. Vacant units are foot-patrolled twice each night. I'd know if there was something like that. Not a chance."

We talk across the cruiser hood. A familiar brown bag with red, yellow, brown printing lays crumpled on the front seat. A paper cup of fresh coffee steams in the holder projecting from the dash.

"I'm not looking to cause you trouble, son."

He straightens. "No trouble, sir. This is my job."

"Unless I have to. I've been here over an hour and this isn't my first time. No patrol cars. No foot patrols. Two kids doing the hump in a unit up the next block. They didn't look worried about being interrupted either."

Meg and I had nearly been doing the same thing. I think briefly how Meg would respond to the patrolman's flashlight shone in her face mid-thrust and try not to laugh.

"Maybe you were looking for company in the coffee shop. I don't blame you. Or one of the pubs along Queen Street. I could ask if anyone's seen you there, pass it on to, who is it?" I look again at the crest on the cruiser's door. "Blaine Security? But that's a lot of work for me and trouble for you. I'd rather just talk to some of the kids who kip in here."

He fumes. He hasn't done two years of community college Law and Security courses to eat shit from some old bastard poking about his watch. He hasn't done it to lose his first ten dollar an hour job, complete with uniform and gear, either.

"Fucking company doesn't understand you have to work with people. Two guys can't begin to keep a site this size secure on their own."

"I understand."

"Work our ass off to keep squatters and kids out of the open sites, then find some kids have keys."

"Keys? How would they get keys?"

"Like someone would tell me. We put in our watch reports the locks need changing but nothing happens. We tell the office, they say don't worry about it. It's not even the same house. Different ones as finished units are sold and new ones are built. How am I supposed to do my job if the owners don't care who has keys?"

"Which one now?"

"For a month or so it's been number 23 on Fairlane. That's over there." He gestures off his left shoulder. "Haven't found them yet this weekend, but if it hasn't been sold, that's where they'll be."

"Just weekends?"

"Mostly. Since summer."

"I'm looking for a girl about fifteen, maybe younger. Hair dyed spikey red."

"That's pretty vague." Now he's showing off his college training. "Height? Complexion?" I oblige with what I can remember. "There's one kid like that. Haven't seen her this weekend."

"What about her friends?"

"Some of them hanging outside number 23 Fairlane on Friday. It was late and they hadn't gone inside so I chased them off."

"Where to?"

"I don't know. Around. I see some cleaning car windows over at Coxwell and Lakeshore sometimes."

"Can you let us into 23 for a look around?"

He shakes his head. "I don't have a key."

I nod, smile. "You sure? So much for the twice nightly foot patrols, eh?"

"Davis has the keys. He's way over the other side of the survey. You want to wait till he gets to Fairlane, be my guest."

"Key'd be pretty handy when you want a little taste yourself." He scowls. "How about it, ever trade a warm place to sleep for bit of kid-die-poon?"

"Fuck you." He's in his car and squealing away, shooting dust and grit in his wake.

On a cold night it's a long walk over to the intersection he named, with nothing to block the fall wind off the lake.

"Good night officer," Meg says as we start the walk. "How did you know he spends part of his shift in the pubs?"

"Didn't for sure. Night watch is thrilling as eight hours of Oprah. Pays lousy. Any time I've found a security guard on site, he's got a hobby, usually a book. Our guy's front seat had donuts and coffee, but no reading material. I figured I'd push that button first."

"If it hadn't worked?"

"Push another one."

XIV

It's a long walk to the corner of Lakeshore and Coxwell, only a bit shorter through the fields waiting to be consumed by construction, nothing but a strip of aging willows between us and the wind coming in off the lake.

"Tell me about last night," I ask Meg to distract her from the cold.

"You really don't remember?"

"Nothing after dinner. I remember you paying the bill, giving the waiter your card, but I don't remember leaving your fancy restaurant."

"The restaurant was emptying as we left. We were late back to The Farm. Later, you said, than you would normally be. We should have skipped it entirely."

I remember thinking the eighty-six twenty for the red nightie was the best money I've spent, even if she didn't wear it for very long. I should be whining now about how little rest I got. If you think energetic sex with a beautiful woman is the mid-life fantasy of a fat, aging ex-cop, you're right. I'd really like to see what Meg can do with a little bit of nylon.

"But we slipped in for the last race. They didn't charge admission."

"They don't after ten." Cecil was at one of the snack booths, sharing a few words with a man dressed entirely in black, with black hair and sunglasses. They saw us and parted.

"Who's that with Cecil? Do you know him?" Meg asked.

"Name's Sweetie Mack. Styles himself a professional gambler. Do we have to be here tonight? The Farm will still be here tomorrow."

"And the bed will still be in the hotel when we get there later. I'm having a good time John. Don't spoil it."

Cecil walked straight out the door without even looking at us. Made me feel good. The man in black followed Meg and I into the smokers' lounge. We were safe. No sign of Toby or the kid.

"Hi again," Crouch said to Meg as we sat.

I said. "Anything good for tonight?"

"At Campbellville?" he asked.

"Anywhere. If I make just one bet, what should it be?"

He frowned at his racing form covered in notes and scribbles. Malcolm was there. The woman he was eyeballing in the afternoon was at another table, one leg coiled around a guy wearing a tan fedora. Toohey, a friend of Crouch's, was at our table and Ivan the Russian, so skinny his shadow has a spine. I asked them all the same thing.

"You're feeling lucky?" Crouch observed.

"Blessed, that's me. Too good to spend the entire night with a bunch of assholes like yourselves. Places to go, things to do." Girlfriends to see in red nighties.

"Assholes?"

"You've missed the triactor."

"Assholes?"

"All right, I apologize for that. Should have said, 'Gentlemen such as yourselves.' I don't want anything complicated. I'm not going to be here long. Don't roll anything over or shit like that. A straight bet."

They didn't, or wouldn't. Crouch and Ivan flipped their eyebrows and burrowed back into their paperwork. Malcolm threw his down in disgust.

"What about you, Sweetie? Can you show these guys up?" I asked.

"Three hundred is hardly worth the trouble," the man in black answered. He was sitting at the next table, trousers with keen-edged creases, shoes shiny, shirt open at the neck to show his gold chain and medallion. A black raincoat was folded on the chair next to him. His black hair was brushed straight back.

"It's all the trouble I can afford, Sweetie. Come on. Show me you can pick a winner."

He took off his sunglasses, leaned over and said: "If you'd gotten here earlier, I could have suggested Makin' Mojo. That's a three year old placed at Woodbine an hour ago. Nobody expected him in the money this early."

"Yet you're still here," I pointed out. "You'd be home in your PJs if there weren't something worthwhile left on the form. Come on. Show me you can predict more than the past."

He looked down at the open page of his handicapping sheet. "How much money do you think I'd be worth if someone like you could goad me into doing what I don't want to do, eh?" He pulled his lips back like he'd tasted something bad, and shifted his weight away.

"Toby and Gretchen have gone," I say to Malcolm. "Thank god."

"She left right after you this afternoon. Probably gone back to her Mama. Toby didn't even notice she was gone. Ran out an hour ago, all upset. What's he expect? The kid's fifteen. What's there for her to do here all afternoon?"

"He probably tell her this is video game parlour." Ivan the Russian was sprawled out from his seat, long legs stretched under our table and part of Sweetie's.

"Ready to go?" Meg asked.

"What, now that Cecil's gone you don't want to hang around anymore?"

"I thought you wanted to go."

"That was then. Now I'm looking for a bet."

I bought a fresh program for Woodbine. Meg furrowed her brows. I wrote numbers down the right-hand margin like they meant something. I underlined some words and phrases with a pencil that came with the form. I looked up and caught Malcolm and Crouch trying to crib from my sheet. I smiled, turned away, made a few extra marks, took Meg by the elbow and followed to the parimutuels a minute to post time. Crouch and Ivan jumped and followed, racing past when we got out the door.

"I sort of like number three," she said. I shrugged an *if you think so*. "Sweetie's a gambler? Did you get information from him?"

"Don't even know for sure he's Sweet," I said.

"Maybe I'll bet twenty on my horse, and twenty on yours," Meg said.

"Don't bet them both to win." Meg rolled her eyes. Did I think she hasn't been to a track before?

I only bet the one race. I lost. Meg won again. We bought drinks from Wally and somehow time passed.

That was Saturday put together. We'd been slow getting started after our late-night Friday, ending at the housing development. By the time we got to The Farm Saturday it was noon or later. We found Toby and Gretchen there. Then we left and did some shopping, followed by dinner in the Beaches. I'd seen Neville and Cartwright at the pub. Eventually we'd wandered back to The Farm and here we were.

Somebody bought us a round. I tried to picture Meg in her red nightie, cursed myself for not leaving when I'd had the chance. It was after midnight before I got her out of there. Couldn't have been much later when I almost stepped into Toby, dead in the hotel parking lot.

✦ ✦ ✦

Cities all over have passed bylaws to chase youthful enterprise from street corners, but in Toronto there's still one kid at Lakeshore and Coxwell trying to squeegee a living tonight. I wouldn't have thought this a good corner to work, but I watch him do about two windows each red light at probably a buck a go, average. The low crotch on oversized green workpants make for a sort of stutter-gait when he sidles up to traffic before it stops moving, then circles aggressively and barks thanks when a window rolls to drop coins in his palm. Two hours would buy some groceries and leave enough to get high. And there's room for more kids on the corner. Must be the bylaw keeps competition away.

I'm wrong about another thing, too. This is no kid. He looks mid-twenties. Could be older than the security guard in the Olde Woodbine Estates. Or maybe Squeegee Boy just isn't aging well. He has a thin-line beard that runs temple to temple, under his chin and around his mouth. Snazzy, if it had been trimmed in a mirror. He dresses in layers, the top a grey, wool, zipped sweater knocked out at the elbows. He's cut two fingers off the right hand of his wool gloves. These aren't the clothes I saw under Gretchen on the floorboards Friday night, but every city is a collection of communities with turf in common. He could know her.

I get no answers showing a blue sinker. "What do you care, she's a wannabe from the suburbs," I say and bump it to a tenner.

"I make as much in ten minutes." He trots back into traffic.

"And I could go phone the cops to make a complaint about how you do it," I say, but he's not impressed. "How much then?"

"Fifty and we go someplace warm."

"Fifty," I say to Meg. Her brow pinches into wrinkles at the bridge of her nose. Looks cute on her. I almost say, "Just be glad he's not asking for hundreds," but stop because if he hears that, he might. "This is your project," I tell her.

Squeegee Boy lifts a wiper and scrubs squirrel shit from a late-model Buick. Meg gives him twenty bucks when he comes back to the curb.

"The rest after we hear what you have to say." He nods. I'm impressed. Meg's a fast study.

Squeegee Boy hides his full pail behind a billboard with six feet of cleavage on a blond teenybopper in mid squirm. "PUNCH MUCH" it says in a typeface I've never seen my side of a cereal box. I'm too old for advertising. We walk the two blocks north and snug into Java Hut.

"What's your name?" Meg asks while we wait our turn at the counter.

"Doggo," he says.

"Doggo what?"

He giggles and orders extra large, double-double.

"Wait," he says when I push a bill to the coffee-grunt, "I'm not done," and he orders a box of Minnie 'Nuts, small, sugar-dusted donuts. We pick a table and sit, me next to Squeegee Boy, or Doggo, Meg across the table. Java Hut is your classic fluorescent-lit space. All the comfort that plastic can provide. Doggo keeps the box of donuts to his side of the Formica tabletop. He doesn't believe that shit about the communal breaking of bread.

"So, yeah, there's a Gretchen came down weekends. Got high, got banged, went back home when her allowance ran out."

"Where's home?"

"This is where I earn my other thirty," he says.

"Nope," shaking my head. "This is where I test to see if what you say matches what I already know."

"Markham."

"Markham's a big place."

"Markham's all I know. She never invited the gang up for a pajama party. Her old man's something in real estate up there. I heard that."

"He's something down here."

"Not so much. He's into the new survey on the old track, but that doesn't put him in the big leagues downtown. Moving forward, though."

Doggo makes me laugh. "What, you're the biz wiz of Lakeshore Road?"

He stiffens. "I read the financial section when I find it laying around. Anyway, move forward is what they all do, isn't it?"

"Gretchen doesn't invite you to Markham, but she keeps open house down here."

"You heard about that? Yeah, she had keys for a vacant house all summer. Par-ty time."

"Daddy's an understanding guy."

"Maybe. Or he thinks she's out of control, wants to be sure she sleeps safe. There's security guards there can keep an eye on her." Meg opens a fresh pack of cigarettes, lights one up. "You should quit those things. They'll kill you," Doggo says.

Meg blows smoke over our heads. She leaves the cigarettes on the table.

"You talk about her in the past tense."

"Yeah, so?"

"Like she isn't around anymore."

"Not around me. Not for weeks."

"What happened?"

"People move along, you know."

Meg starts looking around the room. I scoop a tinfoil tray from the next table. She flicks ash, takes another drag and blows out, lips skewed to avoid sending smoke into our faces.

"Her father was killed Saturday night."

"No shit?" He shakes his head, then smiles. "That should get things jumpin' up on the moraine."

His coffee is gone already. He waggles his cup for more. I put a toonie on the table and Meg goes to the counter.

"You're thinking about her stepfather. Her real father delivered diapers for a living."

"Gretch never mentioned him," he says. "Fits though, eh? The evil stepdad bit. Whaddya know?"

"You ever meet him?"

He shakes his head. "Who needs to meet a guy delivers diapers?"

"The stepfather."

"I did once, yeah. I'm over by the Beaches library, she and this sleek dude, Ray Bans, shiny suit, step out of a limo. He's a type, you know, combs out the Grecian Formula to show a little grey at the temples. She spots me and makes introductions, like she's rubbing me in his face. I mean, back then I was humping her all weekend and here I'm shaking hands with her old man. And then I'm thinking, what puts a suburb kid on the downtown streets, you know? Usually a funny uncle or somebody back home, get what I mean? So I'm shaking hands with the guy who's maybe doing her back home through the week, and maybe she's rubbing him in my face, like. Weirded me right out, man. Completely. I hadda cut her loose."

"How old? How tall?"

He makes a show of thinking. "Now I'm earning my other thirty."

I was hoping he'd forget that till after he spilled. Then we could at least deduct the donuts. Meg gives him another twenty and looks to me. I cough the crumpled tenner I'd flashed earlier at the street corner.

"Shorter than me by a bit. Five nine, ten. Coming up on forty but working hard to look thirty, know what I mean? Doing a lifestyle that'll make him look sixty when he's fifty."

"You're a big help."

"I'm telling you he's a type. Fuck. Guys like him play macho all day on Bay Street then throw up a C-note to get their asses spanked over the hoods of their Beamers by a hot young trannie down at SkyDome parking lot. All the fucking same, these guys."

"How would you know?" Meg, back with the coffee, asks.

"It's a steady source of coin. For some."

"But not for you," Meg says.

"Hey, I'm strictly street legal. One hundred per cent, guaranteed legit." He sits up straight, scans the traffic outside. "Unless you count the occasional piece of underage poontang."

"Did you see Gretchen this weekend?"

"Nope. But I wouldn't now we're no longer"—he makes little quotation marks with the first two naked fingers on each of his gloved hands—"an item."

"Who's she with now?"

"Anything with a dick. But I tell you, there's this one kid been following her down weekends from the 'burbs. He's got it bad, but he ain't getting any, see what I mean."

"What's his name?

"Jason."

"Jason?"

"If he told me his last name, I wouldn't remember it. You're gonna go looking, you can't miss him. He's the whole ball of wax, square jaw, crewcut, shirt with big numbers on it."

"A jock."

"Oh yeah, but he ain't the quarterback. He's more the guy hangs with the quarterback, know what I mean? He's the guy gets the shit kicked out of him keeping three-hundred pound slobs off the quarterback. Brains in his sneakers. See this donut?" He holds up one of the Minnies Meg bought him at the counter. "This donut would be Jason's brain," he pauses for effect, "if the hole was bigger."

"What's this I see here, jealousy?"

He pulls his shoulders back, slumps in the moulded plastic chair. "Lately he's been giving the quarterback a rest, dogging Gretch around weekends. She acts like it's cute, ignores him then waits while he catches up. I'm not much on cute, myself. You're looking to find him, just ask for Gretchen's Jason."

"Where would I look?"

A rivulet of condensed water drips down the window behind his head. Outside, the sky has been black a couple hours.

"Man, you don't quit." He shakes his head. I slide my chair his way, lean to press him in to the glass. "There's a rave in a parking ramp under the Gardiner, around Cherry. Been shaking all weekend. You might get lucky. It's Gretchen's scene."

He stands when I free him up. "I think you got more than fifty bucks worth."

I agree. "Two coffees and a box of donuts more."

He looks around, pockets Meg's smokes. "Thanks. I got friends on the weed."

"We should check to see we've still got our shorts," Meg says after he's gone.

I get coffees to go for us both.

"You're going back to the room now?" she says on the sidewalk, smiling.

Doggo isn't headed back to his corner like he said he would. He's turned east instead. I turn the same way.

"Shouldn't we be going to the rave?"

"I didn't get that. What's a rave?" I ask.

"Like a dance, only thousands of dancers, all ages. Usually in a warehouse or other big vacant space. Lights, DJs. Non-stop music. Big speakers."

I look at her, don't know what to say. How does she know this shit?

"I was at one, a fundraiser for St. Joe's hospital. Usually the location is a secret until the last minute. We didn't do that, of course, but otherwise it was a blast."

I find myself checking shop windows, drives, alleys as we go by. An ex-cop thing; it's all I can do not to rattle the doorknobs. Most places are closed. Sunday-night quiet. There was a couple in a sleeping bag at the streetcar turn-round back by the corner. Two girls sharing fruit juice in a variety store doorway. Not much life on the street.

"If the location's a secret, how does anyone know to go?" I ask.

"Posters are put up with a number to call the night of the rave, or it's on the Internet, people who sign up to a list get an e-mail. Phone trees. I call eight people and they call eight people and they call eight friends. All that sort of thing, more like a spontaneous party than an organized dance, which is why they wouldn't go for that part at the fundraiser, but otherwise it was the real thing. And, you know, if it's secret, the wrong kind of people stay away."

"People like us," I figure.

We pass the Italian café where I have vague memories of a late night snack. It's closed. Weed-cracked asphalt fills the next lot. I hear Doggo's know-it-all whine from a phone booth outside the closed liquor store.

He has the booth door open so the light isn't on. We've come up on him from behind. I go over and put my fist in his kidneys. He coughs, drops, pukes on my shoes. I grab his collar, swing him out of the booth, fist the phone.

"I'm sorry. You're friend's just been ill. Would you like me to put him in a cab?"

It's a male voice. "No I...sick you say...what?"

"Where should I send him, your address?"

The line goes dead.

I drag Squeegee Boy deeper along the side of the liquor store, away from the lights. "Okay, the rest of it, the part about Gretchen's old man, and no bullshit about which one."

He wipes his lips with the back of his glove. "I told you I don't know her old man."

I smack him twice, flat handed, at the temples. "Come on, come on. Stepdad. He's not helping her with a place in the city. What do you take me for? Rent-a-cops in Olde Woodbine had to figure Gretchen out for themselves. They're sure as fuck not looking out for her welfare."

I prop him against the wall, bring my fist back. His arms come up.

"Okay. He figures she's down here puttin' out for the homies anyways, might as well make herself useful."

"Useful how?"

"She buys a few grams every trip."

"How much?"

"Couple grand."

"That's dealing."

"Yeah, must have a lot of happy friends in junior high."

I hit him low, emptying the rest of his stomach.

"Stop playing me for an asshole. Two grand a week for the kids in class?"

He comes up for air. "All right. She said it was for her old man. He has parties for his developer pals, people he needs favours from, approvals, jobs done faster, shit like that. What she said, honest."

"Why would she tell you?"

It's a shit-faced grin, spittle dripping at the corner. "You know the young ones. Give them a bit of attention, you get their fucking life stories. So little to tell, they gotta say it over and over until it ain't worth what you're gettin' to listen anymore." I bring my fist back again. "All right all right. Don't hit me. Look, my idea at first was to put her on the street. She laughed, already had a job, making home deliveries. Her old man was afraid of getting pinched making his own buys. Said it would be too embarrassing, ruin his business reputation. But if she got caught he was just another suburban dad with a spoiled kid."

"What did she buy?"

"Blow mostly," he says. "Grass, meth. Not rock."

"Jesus," I say, "what's wrong with the old ways of keeping politicians and planning departments in line? Contribute to election campaigns, set up cushy jobs on boards of directors when they retire. Why fuck with dope?"

"Yeah, see that's what I figured. Everybody does that old stuff, he told me. These days you gotta have an edge."

"Told you? When would he tell you anything?"

"I already told you. Outside the library. Making conversation."

"You've got his phone number. That's who you called just now, right? To tell him I was snooping around asking questions about Gretchen. Right?"

I dig into his pockets, come up with my fifty. The bills are damp. He protests. "Aww, come on man."

"You're her supplier. Should have told me that in the coffee shop."

"Aw, no. Come on."

A couple of slaps. "You're the one selling dope to Daddy. She's the mule."

"No way man! Would I be down washing windshields on a cold Lakeshore corner if I was dealing? Think about it. It doesn't make sense."

"It does if that's where your clients know to find you."

I've let him get rested, confident, don't notice his recovery until too late. His arm comes up and around. I can only lean back, raise my hand, feel the sharp heat of flesh opening. Keep backpedalling, ready for the follow-up, but he legs it out the alley, car horns blaring as he snakes across traffic then takes off down the other side, trailing curses. "Careful, he's got a knife," I say to no one who can hear. Toby was killed with a knife, I think. Silent. Bloody.

Always carry a clean handkerchief, Miss Meyers taught me back in grade one. Never know when you'll be in an alley fight and need to stanch a wound.

"Did you need to hit him like that," Meg asks when I step back on the street.

XV

If I go get my hand stitched, I'll be sitting in a hospital waiting room till the cock crows. I'd rather be in bed with Meg when that happens. I get her to tie the handkerchief tight, keep my hand in a fist until the blood stops running. It just about does when the Queen streetcar arrives. We go west, using the night to track down Gretchen at her rave.

Storefronts I'd seen empty on my last trip along Queen East now house small art galleries, antique shops and design studio start-ups, making the strip clubs and the non-franchised donut shops seem even seedier than before. More people too, on the green grass intervals that squint by the streetcar window, pushing their lives in bundle buggies and shopping carts. A slight girl in a sleeveless purple top and tan shorts pulls a toddler away from curious pedestrians, toward two adults zonked on a park bench.

It's too fucking cold for shorts and I'm too fucking tired to care. Gretchen should be home in Markham, the family running interference with the cops. I could be worrying about that, but Doggo hadn't mentioned Markham as a possibility for finding Gretchen. He said raves were her scene. Of course, Doggo is a liar. But he's our only source regarding Gretchen's whereabouts. Besides, we're nowhere near Markham, and my chevy's in the pound. Public transit will get us to the rave, not Markham on a Sunday night.

The streetcar clangs past a 24-hour pharmacy. I pull the stop-cord, get off for bandages and antiseptic. A couple of chocolate bars for energy.

"You knew he was lying," Meg says when we catch the next streetcar and I fill her in.

"Everybody lies when they talk to the cops."

"You're not a cop anymore," she says.

"Think Doggo appreciates the difference?"

I'm yanked forward by the streetcar suddenly braking. The rave isn't really under the Gardiner Expressway, and it's not really in a parking ramp. It's at a vacant plant in the industrial sector of Toronto Harbour.

Thousands of kids homed in on the din pumping out of the old building like it's a giant speaker box. We're only looking for one, a fifteen-year-old girl with short, red, spiked hair named Gretchen. She won't stand out in this crowd.

The ground grumbles a rock 'n' roll beat, except it's way faster than I remember. Meg says it's industrial/techno. Sounds right. She chatters at some of the kids passing on the sidewalk. They seem to think it's cool people our age go to raves. I tell them we operate the Twist demonstration booth on the second floor. They seem to think it's cool people our age operate a Twist demonstration booth at a rave. They're polite, mostly, trained early to appreciate peace, order and good government if that means waiting patiently in line to cough up twenty bucks for a Sunday night out.

Even in the fall chill there's acres of exposed teen flesh. Sound throbbing from the old plant provides a sort of sexual friction, like being hit by waves from a giant, ultra-sonic vibrator. We take a place in the line along Cherry Street, several hundred feet before the break in the barbed wire topped fence that I take to be the entrance.

A metric tonne of beefcake hovers just inside the gate, surrounding a couple of tables set up to control entry and collect cash. They wear black sweatshirts with SECURITY printed in white, capital letters across the back. They pat down each raver as he/she enters. A gaggle of Metro's finest lingers over steaming coffee cups to the side of the building.

"Cops and security staff, and a lot of both," I shout to Meg, and repeat it when she doesn't hear.

"Gotta have 'em," the kid next in line answers. "City says, or no event permit. They don't do nothing, so it's okay. Don't hassle them, they leave you alone, 'less you start waving a gun around or something."

"You let the private security bulls pat you down?" I ask.

"It's not so bad. Takes only a few secs. I just don't think about it."

"Not so bad for you," says a girl turning from the line ahead of us. She's black, has long, blond hair hanging straight down her back. Red elastic around her top half, a pretty navel winking like a cylcops, and silver-blue pants flaring over white, clunky-heeled shoes that project her ass and what she's got struggling inside the red elastic. And she's cold. I can tell.

"Yeah," one of her friends joins in, "you don't have Cro-Magnon Man copping a feel every time you want to party."

"Well, maybe," the first kid again. He squirms uncomfortably. "You think the real cops wouldn't do that?"

"I know they do," red elastic says, flipping an imaginary strand of hair over her shoulder. Her friends are attractive young ladies too, but she's the star.

"Careful," Meg warns them. "This guy's an ex-cop."

More heads turning our way. "Here for a free, nostalgic squeeze?"

I shake my head. "Hardly. Never pulled extra duty at one of these things. Spent most of my years dicking it."

"Is that what you do after copping a free feel?" says red elastic.

"Detective."

"Ho, yeah? Like undercover? Ever shoot anybody?" It's always one of the first questions.

"Tell you a story," I say and the kids gather closer in—a touching display of respect for an authoratative elder. Goes some way to explain why they'd rather be groped by strangers than give up their boogie nights.

"When I started the job, I partnered with a guy named Sherk."

I look to Meg for the recognition in her eyes.

"Time that comes to mind is Christmas Eve, early 70s. We pulled a plain wrapper and Sherk drove. Did some follow-ups, mostly routine. Hit business strips to collect some seasonable greetings. Christmas is usually quiet, so I didn't squawk when Sherk turned the squadie south on Wentworth."

"What's Wentworth?" a voice asks. "Like a street?"

I tell where we're from and he loses interest. A bad place, his parents have told him, polluted and full of losers.

"I knew where he was going," I continue. "Almighty One Towing had a yard up on the edge of the city. Every Christmas they put out a big spread for their drivers and favourite cops."

Meg doesn't quite believe it. "Almighty One Towing?"

"Yeah. You gotta dig it. Your car's in the ditch, your ass is on asphalt and out of the night comes a three-hundred pound, stogie-chomping, gospel-spouting, grease-shining behemoth in a tow truck. He's got you on the hook before your pupils stop spinning round your eyeballs. People let Apostle Ronnie drag them miles out of town to a backyard body shop on his word that the bondo-rat who scuttles out his home workshop is an honest Christian with thirteen mouths to feed."

"The family values pitch way back then, huh?"

This is the kid who first spoke to us. I let the "way back then" dig pass.

"Oh yeah. Of course, what Apostle Ronnie always failed to mention was that the mouths had been fathered with as many different women across the continent and the fender-slapper had no idea where most of them were. Only one mouth ever got reliably fed and that was Apostle Ronnie's. He recommended repair shops based on the size of their tax-deductible donation back to the Almighty One Church of the Holy Hook."

"You're making this up," Meg says.

"No, it was the Almighty One Church of the Holy Cross. We changed Cross to Hook because Ronnie was forever hooking new parishioners. It wasn't a straight-up scam, though. I have seen Apostle Ronnie take a tailgate testament, get a signed statement directing leftover body parts to ailing Christians, and ease a lead-foot's soon-to-be vacant carcass toward salvation ten minutes before the first ambulance pulled up."

"Hallelujah." A cynic.

"Ronnie did his good works, but it didn't hurt that the business name put him near the top in the phone directory either. Plus, as I say, every Christmas Eve he laid out a spread for patrolmen in this chapel he had set up in his tow yard office. Rolls, hot ham, roast beef, Swedish meatballs, pizza. Cases and cases of rye."

"Booze?"

"Ronnie didn't indulge himself, but he wouldn't deny good men in blue who kept the streets safe and sent many wretches on the path to

Almighty One Towing by calling him first to the accident. All the tow companies did something for the cops, but Apostle Ronnie's was best. Long as you brought along a plush toy he was collecting for the poor kids.

"Things were a bit more open then. Nobody said anything if you went to Ronnie's end of shift, and the bottles went home sealed. Except who's going to tell if a few guys came in before shift ended or some of the bottles got opened early?

"Sherk drove out for lunch break. It was an evening shift. Sherk had three drinks before time to go back on-call and I couldn't move him. So I sat in the cruiser to monitor the radio. Make like we're on duty even if we weren't. Like I said, Christmas Eve, not much doing, but eventually there had to be something. It came as a disturbing-the-peace call at a house just blocks from the tow yard. We were closest, supposedly on duty and I couldn't think of any reason to give for not taking it."

The line into the rave shuffles ahead a few feet, taking us with it. Then attention comes back to me.

"I could have taken someone else but it was Christmas. I'm not going to spoil somebody's time because I can't quiet a noisy house party. So I go alone. Five minutes later I'm banging the door of this wood-frame cottage. There's shouting from somewhere in the back. The door opens and I show my badge. Must be thirty people inside this pillbox. 'There's been a complaint,' I say. 'Yeah? Somebody call the cops?' the guy who answered the door yells back over his shoulder.

"There's a kitchen in back, where most of the noise is coming from. I go in. Beer bottles on the table and across the tiny bit of counter, empties in the sink. One guy doing all the shouting, small, skinny, spitting nails and threatening to hammer somebody. Another guy, pretty big, is sitting in a kitchen chair, the ring around his left eye getting darker and thicker as I watch. It'll be a dandy shiner come Christmas morning, but that looks to be the worst of it. Three, four other guys taking turns patrolling the little space there is between these two and squeezing out to the living room where the wives are parked. Everyone trying to be real casual. 'Nothing going on here officer.' Kids being shushed everywhere.

"Only one woman in the kitchen and she's pissed. She's wearing a tiny black skirt, a red sparkly blouse over bullet tits. Her hair's permed in tight circles and her face is cigarette cracked. A sixty-year-old puss on top a thirty-year-old body with a skirt makes me think of Jos. Louis' half-moon cakes every time she turns around.

"'Arrest him,' she says. She means the little nail spitter.

"'It's Christmas Eve. You want me to arrest him?' I say, and she does, but everybody else turns away.

"I compromised, took him out, put him in the back of the cruiser. Only I had a problem. Couldn't take him to the station because someone would ask where was Sherk. Couldn't put him back in the house, either, not straight away. I got his ID, fussed with paperwork, let him cool in the back seat, all the while wondering is this better or worse than hanging around Apostle Ronnie's rest of the shift. Eventually he tells me his brother, the big guy, was coming on to his girlfriend. The girlfriend is the woman with the perm and her ass hanging out her skirt. I must have given him a look, because he says 'I know, I know, but she can tie the ribbons on a Christmas present with just her tongue.'

"He's funny and it's Christmas so I give him a choice. I can drive him home, or he can go back inside and behave. He says the cottage *is* home, so it wasn't really any choice at all.

"What I should have done, I should have driven him outside the city, let him out on a side road miles from trouble. But I thought it's Christmas, what the hell, so I walked him back up to the house, told them inside that if Leon was good, could he come back in. 'Sure,' they all said, 'no problem. Give us Leon back.'"

"So what's Sherk up to when you get back to Apostle Ronnie's?" Meg asks.

"Wait, you're getting ahead. I'm hardly at the foot of the steps before there's shouting again and the sounds of furniture breaking. I don't knock, go straight in and through to the kitchen. The table's on its side, Leon is slicing the air with one of the legs he's torn loose. Everyone else is backed into the corners. I bring out the sap, wait for the table leg to pass by and crack Leon on the elbow. Everyone hears the bone crunch. The room goes quiet. Leon hollers, drops to the floor.

"Now everyone's out of the woodwork. Women crowd in behind me from the living room. 'What'd I do that for?' 'Cop brutality.' Someone says I should have let them talk to Leon first. Nobody was talking when he had the table leg, but that's history now. It's so close in there I haven't the elbow space to defend myself. Hands start pulling at the tools on my belt and then big brother with the shiner shouts, 'Nobody hits my son of a bitch little brother and lives till Boxing Day.' Couple of shoves and I lam out the back way.

"But I'm not out of trouble. I'm in a roofed porch that runs across the back of the cottage, full of all kinds of shit, garbage pails, newspapers, lawn chairs. Coloured Christmas lights strung on nails, yards and yards across the outside. I find the steps down and jump, only I catch a string of lights under my chin and like that I'm on my ass looking up at stars. Some of them are my own. Each porch step where I've landed is a line of pain across my back. Shouting from the kitchen door brings me around. Leon's friends are doing a Curly-Larry-Mo all trying to get through the door at once.

"I get up and limp around the yard, lights dragging behind like I'm some monster lawn ornament chased to the castle by angry townspeople. I can't find a way out. The yard's a box, must be eight feet high, fenced from the neighbours' sides. It's open from the house to the garage but more of Leon's people are coming out the side door and up the drive. I finally find a wood picnic table behind the garage. First step on the bench, second on the top, it's enough to vault the fence."

"Bullshit," red elastic girl says, looking me up and down.

I wouldn't mind putting my finger in her brown navel. What'll Meg think if I ask the girl's name? "Hey, I was in pretty good shape back then. Getting over was no problem, but that was it. Suddenly I was stopped."

"Wait, I've heard this before. You ran out of electricity," the girl says.

"No. Most of the lights were still on but the cord was caught on top of the fence, or the picnic table, somewhere. I'm dangling sideways on the other side of the fence, one foot inches from the ground, waiting for Leon's friends and relatives to come around and do me like a Christmas pinata. Then there's barking. I look down, at this fucking little terrier going at my ankle. Saved my fucking life."

The line moves ahead a bit more. The girl in red spandex doesn't say anything, but she doesn't give up the attitude either.

"Dog's owner heard the barking, came out with a machete. About a yard of gun-metal blade. Starts whacking the top of the fence.

Fingers and elbows disappear back over the other side just ahead of the blade. The guy's about six foot, and shrinking. Hasn't shaved in days. He's in house slippers and a buttoned sweater. He picks up his dog and heads back to his house.

"'Hey, wait. What about me?' I asked.

"'What about you?' he says back. 'I'm thinking you should hang there while you consider what makes you any different from the rest of that rabble.'

"'Police,' I say.

"'You're the one's supposed to protect us around here?' he asks. 'You look like any old idiot with his ass in a sling to me.'

"Looking up, I see that the top of the fence is all chewed, cuts and nicks one end to the other. 'You've done this before,' I say.

"'Guess I can credit you for getting here before anyone got shot. For once.' He sizes things up and takes a whack with his machete. Drops me like harvesting bananas. 'Come on. I'll put you back on your horse.'

"There's half a bottle of five-star cognac on his kitchen table. A drained glass beside it. He gets another glass from his cupboard and fills them both.

"He says I'll feel like shit in the morning.

"'Feel like shit right now,' I told him, and poured myself another. There was only a heel in the bottle when I told him I had to get back to work."

The kids' attention shifts as we shuffle closer to the entrance in the fence.

"I'm not finished," I tell them. "Cleaned myself up best I could. It was getting to end of shift when I got back to Apostle Ronnie's. Sherk met me at the door.

"'So old Boot invited you to a Majors' Family Christmas, did he?'

"'Who in fuck is old Boot?' I asked.

"'Sergeant Rolland Boothby, retired thirteen years from the force,' Sherk says. 'The guy we got to call in the complaint. The guy who saved your ass. Consider yourself initiated.'

"I got two slices of bologna, smeared them with mustard, and slapped one on each of Sherk's fat cheeks. Then I made myself the thickest ham sandwich you've ever seen..."

"...and you didn't leave Apostle Ronnie's until the shift was done," Meg finishes.

"Long after."

As a punchline it fizzles. The kids have gone on to dissing each other's wardrobes. Meg catches my silence and speaks to pretend she's been listening. "What is this? A little self-deprecating story to melt a woman's resistance?"

"Is it working?"

"Baloney and mustard? Not so far."

XVI

The heel of a white styrofoam cup is wedged into a fence link behind Meg's left ear. The kids fore and aft turn their attention to paying admission. Across the road is a porridge of cardboard and canvas, a tent city the homeless have pulled together on vacant industrial land, abandoned tonight to the ravers' din.

"I have a headache," I tell Meg when it's our turn to enter.

"The music or the forty dollar admission?" she asks.

I put two twenties on the table. "Forty bucks per," a voice scratches from the cave-mouth on a woman in a blue-and-black lumberjack coat. She's massive, shoulders like Gordie Howe and breasts that pour onto her side of the table. Her hair is a black helmet, streaked grey like she'd squeezed a can of spray paint without checking which way the nozzle was turned. "Or ain't the lady with you?" she asks, the flat experience in her good, grey eye showing she thinks it doubtful. I wonder if they list her bra size in the Victoria's Secret catalogue.

"Both," I answer Meg, laying out a fifty and tenner in exchange for one of my earlier twenties, which I have to pull from the money-hugger's fist. A waif to her right stamps the backs of our hands with a clear fluid that glistens in September moonlight.

"Black-light hand stamps to show we've paid," Meg says.

A pair of the security black-shirts move to pat us down. I hold open my jacket. Meg gets most of their attention. I lose sight of her in the beefcake. They're each big enough to be offspring of the nest queen collecting money at the front gate. If I didn't know better, I'd think Meg was having a good time.

I look at the twenty still in my hand from the exchange at the gate. "Am I confused or did I just pay eighty bucks to watch you get felt up?"

"It's all right John. They're checking for weapons." She takes my arm, starts pulling me toward the music.

"Well in your case, I hope they let you keep them. Christ I'm tired. What did we come here for?"

"I'll look after your headache," she says. "First, finish your Christmas story. There's more to it, isn't there?"

"Yeah. There's a moral. Back up your partner no matter what or he'll hang you out to dry. Sherk's variation on the first rule of police work. Look out for your own."

"We're here to find Gretchen, or anyone who knows her," Meg reminds me.

"Right. I'll begin over here," and I head round the corner where the real cops hide and kibitz at sixty bucks an hour. More of them than I expected. Place has blue shirts up the butt-hole. I describe Gretchen, what she wore yesterday at The Farm: black tights under a Black Watch tartan kilt, a black sweater cut short to let her navel wink at passing punters, gold earrings and a stud on her tongue. Red spike heels that left her ankles bare beneath the tights.

"Anyone like that here?" I ask the boys in blue.

They giggle manfully. "Couple thousand," one says.

The black-shirt squad not fully involved with squeezing passing flesh is only slightly more helpful. They give the same answer, but add "We'll keep an eye out," before showing me their backs. Nothing for it but to go through the haystack ourselves.

Meg catches me at the main entrance, an open truck-bay door. "For your headache," she says, pushing a white pill between my lips with a slender finger. I smell her perfume, give the finger a nibble, ask, "Just one?"

She nods, gives me a chaser of water from the bottle she's bought. We go inside. Music's louder. Didn't think it could be. Lasers flash patterns from the corners. Lights stutter, making it hard to distinguish faces. Meg leads us through clusters of kids stopping to shout in ears, getting head-shakes, sometimes nods. We give off asking while Meg dances. Music never stops, one DJ riffing into the next, scratching vinyl, a string of their own patter runs over the beat.

Crowds of young, tight bodies move lamé in ways that make me want to reach out and touch it. I thrust my hands into my pockets. Meg shimmies back and forth. I want to hold her and watch her at the same time.

"Come on, dance," she says and God help me it sounds like a good idea. I can shake my booty and watch for Gretchen easy as stand around and watch for her. Wonder if the bulge in my pants shows. Fuck it.

Turns out you can Boogaloo to this beat if you want to. Shing-a-ling too. Funky Monkey, Mash Potato, Boney Maroney, Swim, Jerk. Fly. Christ, whodathunk? Until tonight, nobody but Liz ever knew I could dance, at least nobody who hadn't been too polite to laugh. No one laughs here. They move in to see what I'm doing and drift away with their own variations on my steps. Look everybody, I'm Nipsey fucking Russell. We are each a universe unto ourselves, having our own, individual fun, but together in a cosmic, interconnected, family tree of—I'm going to say it—Love. Not *love* exactly, but something like it, a single, pulsating party machine, an entity. One throbbing body with three hundred pounds of sweating gristle, me, way smooth, grooving at the centre. A love machine. I could dance all night, like the song says.

"That the twist?" Someone we'd met on the street asking. How is it she can find us in this crowd but we can't find Gretchen or Jason?

"It's hot. I need a drink," Meg says, waggling the quarter inch of water in the heel of her bottle.

The place is human-heated. I'm dripping. In the line to the water concession, I start asking after Gretchen again. Heads shake. Bummer.

"She hangs weekends in the new housing development over by the Beaches," Meg says.

"She the one guys call 'Gretch the Ketch?'" a voice from behind says.

It's the crush of bodies that keeps me from grabbing her by the lapels. That and she's wearing a black leather halter that has no lapels. Another young, flat, bare belly. I'm beginning to note a fashion trend. Resolve to try it later. Did I say she's young? There are kids here without tits or beards but they've all got navels. Mine is what's commonly called an "innie," meaning you'd have to dig with a shovel to find it, not that anybody ever offers.

"Probably," Meg answers.

"It's stupid because nobody has to chase her," the voice says. Big eyes, pouty lips. Parents, school, television, Santa and life in general are probably her top five disappointments."

"She here?"

Shoulder shrug.

"Who she hang with?" It's my voice. I'm watching myself have this conversation.

Shoulder shrug.

"Anyone else here who knows her?"

Shoulder shrug.

"Look, she was with her father, who died last night." Was it last night? Christ, time has gone all to hell. "Need to find her, make sure she's all right." That too.

"Who are you?"

"Friend of her father's." For sure, me and Toby go all the way back to Friday. "She here?" I'm shouting and it's bringing my headache back, but it's the only way to be heard.

"Might have been. If she was, she was going to leave early."

"Which is it?"

Shoulder shrug. "Don't push. I saw her, but it could be last week, maybe. And early would be, like, one, two o'clock."

"Hey, move up the line, okay? I'm getting, like, real dry back here." I've let about five feet open up between me and Meg. I take the girl in the black halter aside.

"She have friends here?"

"Hey, quit shoving," she says.

"Sorry."

Shoulder shrug. "I told you. She's easy."

"Anyone regular? What about someone named Jason?"

"There's a geek been following her around she said is like from her school."

"In Markham."

Her nod is very pretty: shoulders up, chin down, one time only, for your entertainment pleasure, right here tonight. "It's pathetic. He is such a pooch. The only guy who hasn't been in Gretch's pants."

"Describe him."

She looks out over the crowd, not to spot him, but to show she's above interest in this conversation. "Oh a guy, you know. Blond. Jeans. Wears this green mesh football shirt with the number 66 on it. Very cool in the suburbs. He's too skinny to play football."

"Tall?"

"Taller than me. Shorter than you."

"Gretchen into drugs?" I shout. She makes a face. "More than personal use, I mean. Do you know where she'd get it?" I'm looking to confirm Squeegee Boy, Doggo's information. She sneers. I'm another disappointment visiting from the adult world. "I want to be sure she's safe. Whoever killed her father..."

"Wait, wait, wait. Her father was killed?" She opens her palms to the floor, does a total body shiver. "I do not want any part of this." The crowd absorbs her, like she's gone to visit James Earl Jones in a cornfield.

Meg arrives with three bottles of water. "I thought your friend would want one."

"Turns out we're not friends," I say. I pour the contents of one bottle down my throat, take the lid off a second. "We're looking for a skinny kid, male, blond, medium height, in a green football jersey with the number 66 on it. Gretchen may or may not be here too. Probably not," I decide.

Meg sips her own bottle, nodding. "Up there," pointing to a catwalk running along of a row of blank office windows. At one time managers would have lorded over production workers from that height. "Get a good view of the floor," Meg adds.

I nod into the din. She leads. It takes forever to get to the top, weaving among ravers. And we could be dancing our way up. I'm not sure. My legs are going lead.

Meg writhing on a landing. "How's your headache?"

"Wasn't bad," I say. "Seems on the way back."

She has another pill for me. We reach the top. Faces, moving faces. People stand and sit all along the metal bridge, talking, feet dangling. I try one of the office doors. Locked.

"In use," a kid waiting outside says. "Get in line." He doesn't seem happy about it.

I put my ear to the door. Mumbling. Moaning. Maybe. I give the kid my experienced once-over. He's wearing a football jersey, green mesh. It has a 66 stacked sideways on the front. He's blond. His height appears a touch above average. Why does that seem important? Right! He looks good, part of the big, cosmic family tree. "Gretchen in there, Jason?" I ask him, proud I can remember what I'd been thinking only minutes earlier. I must truly be one of the Great Detectives, capable of any sleutherly feat.

"Who're you?" He's not surprised. He's not angry. He's not afraid.

"Friends of her father's." The secret of successful lying is to keep the story simple and stick to it. "The one was killed last night?" Might have phrased that better.

"I don't think she knows about that yet," Jason says.

"But you do," Meg takes over. We're either side of him.

"It was on TV this morning. I wasn't going to come down to the city this weekend, but..." He didn't finish.

"When you going to tell her?" Meg asks.

"What makes you think she doesn't already know?" I ask.

"I offered to be her witness," Jason says, "if she would only confess her sins to the Lord and repent. I know she will be forgiven."

Repent. Interesting word. Re-pent. To pent again. Gretchen hadn't struck me as the penting kind. "She must laugh you back to Markham."

"I'm not ashamed to declare my faith, to be a beacon in her hour of need. She doesn't know what I mean yet," he admits, "but she will."

"Why don't you take her home to her parents?" Meg's idea. I doubt Gretchen gets taken anywhere she doesn't want to go. That was Toby's trouble, as I recall.

Jason shows the whites of his eyes. "They're not good Christians," he says. "Who are you people? You're not the police. How'd you find me?"

"How 'bout I show you mine if you show me yours?" I try. "What's your last name, Jason? Where were you last night? Anyone can confirm it?"

But Meg has already started: "Your pal Doggo the Squeegee Boy said you might be here."

The faith seems to drain out of him suddenly. He looks surprised, scared, angry all at once. "What's he got..." Again with the unfinished sentence.

The door opens behind me, taking my attention, kids zipping flies, shouldering halter straps. And Jason does a runner, leaves me smiling, feeling really good about our interview, all without reason.

XVII

"He's cute," Meg says.

"He's pathetic," I answer.

"You could have smacked him around a bit," Meg adds, "or don't you do Christians?"

"No, tell the truth, the rare occasion I actually get hold of one."

"What do you call him?"

"A confused kid. Most fundamentalist types don't like to see the rod spared when it comes to kids. Why should I?"

"I couldn't hear it all. Did he say where Gretchen was?"

I shake my head. "He's looking, same as us."

It's hot as hell, my shirt soaked with sweat. We walk the catwalk in front of the bank of offices. We dance. We ask after Gretchen. Time goes. Our investigation doesn't. Meg puts something in my mouth. I pull it out. It's a rubber tit, the kind Liz and I used to honey and give Peggy when she had colic.

"You're grinding your teeth," Meg shouts in my ear.

"Yeah? I snore too, don't you know?" A metal ladder ascends from the catwalk twenty feet into the middle of the ceiling. I put the tit back in my mouth and throw a leg on the first rung. "So long as you're not trying to wean me off the real thing."

The lid comes off the roof at the top of the ladder. I step out onto the flat expanse of tar and pea gravel awash in lights from the city towers to the west. Red tail lights swerve along the expressway. Dark pearl islands necklace the harbour to the south. East where our day began, Toronto looks like the quiet collection of treed neighbourhoods that most of it is. Somewhere down there is our bed at the Beaches Hotel. Somewhere in this city of millions my lonely chevy waits for me to come rescue it. Somewhere Toby's body lies on a slab.

Meg sighs, comes to a decision. "I've been thinking about how we might set things up back home, be in a position to make some money."

"I thought that's what we were doing here."

"It is, but after, there's people I know, Party supporters, others, they've got plans to renovate downtown."

"They've had plans for fifty years. That's why it's fucked in the first place."

"Yes, but money's moving into place. The city is to provide services, build parking ramps." she says. "A big pension fund behind a consortium planning to buy the MacNab Arms."

"IBCW." I spell it out. "International Brotherhood of Construction Workers. It's their pension money, no? That who you want to shake down?"

"Christ no," she flusters. "They'd pour us into pylons on the Red Creek Expressway. They're who you'll be working for. They won't care what else you do, long as you look after their interests well. Very well."

"A house dick."

"Yep."

"Transom peeper."

"That a problem?"

"Fuck no. Get me out of the house. Take pictures of secretaries screwing away their lunch hours."

"If that's how you want to fill the lonely days go ahead, but I was thinking bigger. The Arms is getting a luxury refit. It'll end up very exclusive. Damn near a private club."

"Can't this wait until later? Tonight, we're on the roof, the stars are a-twinkle. So am I." I try the old eyebrow waggle.

"All right. I just thought, the hotel will be a meeting place, where people who make important decisions will roll up their sleeves. And let their hair down."

"A place where the elite meet to cheat?"

"Exactly. And you there to catch them at it, get paid to keep quiet. What do you think?"

I don't think. I'm feeling too good to think business. Lift my arms to the sky, turn circles. "King of the World," I shout to the lights spinning round my head. Meg's laughter reverbs in waves as I turn. I run to each corner of the building, lean out over the prow and shout: "I'm King of the World," then return to Meg hanging close by our porthole back to reality raving below.

"King of the World should take a break," she observes.

I've been looking at these nice, rich kids in their tight clothes and their naked navels all night. I have other ideas, give Meg the eyebrow waggle again. If someone had told me when I was twenty that the eyebrows grow more pliable even as other features stiffen, I'd have said who gives a shit. But look at me now. I take off my clothes. All but my shoes and socks.

"What? On the roof? On gravel?" Meg points out.

I shrug, lie on my back and look at her between the toe-caps of my brogues. "Climb aboard," I offer, ever the gentleman. "King needs nookie."

"I don't think you're actually up for this. Besides, it's too damn cold."

Jeez, she's right. I've assumed *all* of me would be ready, but it isn't so. My pecker lies there like toothpaste squeezed from the tube. Thing is, the pea gravel digging into my back is unbelievable, the best back massage I've ever had and most of mine have been foreplay. The slightest move brings a rush. I cannot fucking believe it. A breeze in off the lake, Meg's hair swirling under a perfect, fall, pinpricked sky, I rock slightly on the roof and the sensation makes my eyes roll.

A head comes through the roof port, watching.

"Gross," it says.

"King of the World," I shout and the head pulls a body through behind it, stepping onto the roof, a glitter of red and blue sequins. More follow, like sparkly lava out a small mountain top. They stand around watching, the music throbbing through the roof membrane like I'm bouncing on speaker felt. Some kids get down beside me on their backs, shirts on and off, some as naked as me for this groovy gravel back massage, stars swimming in our eyes. I have no idea how long we're up there. Meg is dancing with two guys in muscle shirts when the cops arrive.

✦ ✦ ✦

They come through the roof port and more come over the wall from a cherry-picker docked at the side. They grab kids, line them up, pressing with batons. It's a scramble. Feet jump over my prone body, kicking that fabulous gravel in my face. Meg has me by the hair, lifts and pulls me around behind some structure and to the far wall.

"You first," she says. A metal ladder to the ground.

"It's fifty feet," I tell her, "at least."

She throws my clothes over. I step up on the ledge, turn, get a grip and take the first few steps. The rungs make my arches ache. The ladder shifts.

"I don't think this thing's in too good shape," I tell her.

She pushes my head down, gets a leg over. I descend quickly as I can, trying to keep my weight close to the wall, look up long enough to wish Meg had worn a skirt. Could be the angle or the jeans, but her legs look thicker than I thought they were. Maybe balancing on the rungs has her muscles flexed. The ladder shifts again. I watch lag-bolts pull out from the brick. I lean forward, watch them go in again. Close my eyes and keep going, taking it by rote.

You'd think there'd be cops at the bottom waiting for anyone stupid enough to try this route. Turns out one of them had the same thought. I feel his nightstick back of my knee when I'm almost at the bottom. Could be the ladder shifts again, or my hands slip or I just get tired. I let go, laying out the copper like Thanksgiving dinner. He doesn't get up after I do. You might say he's been impressed by my flying tackle. Won't be able to identify me by my clothes, either, though he might have caught a birthmark as it descended on him. Meg gathers up my clothes and I pull the radio from the cop's belt. We hotfoot around behind a second, smaller building. The lot is fully fenced, three strands of barbwire along the top.

The chain-link is secure, but the barbwire hangs down in coils opening a stretch of about five feet near the south corner where the fence turns back toward Cherry. We'll be visible from the street if anyone cares to look, but it's our only shot at getting out. A voice scratches warnings from the radio in my hand: they've found the blue I squished at the bottom of the ladder.

Meg gets over the fence pretty good, but I've got one foot either side, my shoes dug into the links, and my balls dangling loosely against cool galvanized pipe. I remember the black girl in the red spandex top and her assessment of my fence-climbing abilities. Meg throws a rock to get me moving. I'm over the top, but tumble from there. Through an open field of weed-choked asphalt, across Lakeshore and under the expressway, weaving between honking cars, a memorably attractive blond with a naked fat man in tow. Meg hands me my clothes in a thicket of sumac hard by the rail lines.

"I have a confession," she says.

"That wasn't aspirin you gave me for my headache," I guess. I'm not as cold as I would have expected, and not feeling any pain from the falls I've taken. That's two clues right there. There might be others, looking back.

"White Doves. You mad at me?"

"Forget it. Long as we're having fun," I tell her.

She rummages her purse for a cigarette while I dress. Doesn't find one. Catches her breath. The radio scratches at our ears again. Seems the squished cop is up and whining, claims two men jumped him. He's estimated my age, height and weight pretty good. At least he has Meg wrong.

"You shouldn't have jumped on that cop."

I throw her my hurt look. "I fell."

"What's the worst would have happened? We'd have spent the night in jail, paid a fine, been embarrassed. Who'd have cared, really?"

My daughter up in Ottawa already hates my guts, has me down as a cold killer. Tonight would be small potatoes, compared.

"No one. Well, I wouldn't want Sue-Anne spreading this around the neighbourhood."

"Why do you worry about Sue-Anne and them? They're closet swingers themselves," Meg says.

"Sue-Anne?"

"Sue-Anne, Robbie, the whole bunch you met Wednesday night at the restaurant. Not that they actually do much, but it's all they ever talk about. It's all they have in common."

"The night your husband died..."

"Me, Ham and Stan on the dock. I got tired of all the innuendo," she stops, still chasing wind, "the sly double-talk. I told them on the way down to the lake, put up or shut up. It was what Stan wanted, Christ he practically drooled, and Ham, sometimes I think he just married me for show, bait, so he could watch cock get excited. Then I'd be in the way. But nothing happened like usual. I got fed up and went for a swim. When I came back they were side by side, dangling their toes in the water, giggling. It was too childish, so I went up to the cottage. Sue-Anne was on the sofa with Jim Crandall. I doubt she even noticed me go by. So I went to bed. Alone."

I button my shirt, think about all the afternoons and evenings I'd spent trying to get my sleep cycle in sync with rotating shifts, tossing hot sheets in the bedroom while Liz was out, talking with the guy next door. Did she know Robbie was into fucking his friends' wives? Where did she go after I left for work?

Meg goes into traffic, hails a cab, puts me in the back. We're somewhere east of Jarvis. I don't remember getting out again, or climbing the stairs at the hotel, but that's where I wake up.

I dreamed about Liz, sitting in her big armchair watching television as she knitted, her legs curled under her slender, dying body. She asked for a glass of water and I went to the kitchen. The water that came from the taps was brown/green and smelled putrid. I brought tools from the basement and removed the taps, but still the water was bad. Then I was someplace dark trying still but the pipes no longer came apart. Someone laughed and said I needed bigger wrenches, that I could buy them for a week's wages and they took the pipes apart but the water was still bad. I bought a tractor to rip out all the old pipes, a belching Caterpillar big enough to dig beyond the dirty water, to a new, clear, sweet source. When I found it I'd lay clean pipe back to our kitchen, where Liz waited for a glass of water, any water, I didn't need to go to all this trouble. But the tractor kept getting bigger, the sales agent taking for payment my signature and promises I'd deliver clean water to her house first and saying this was their best tractor yet, that it even cleaned ducts. "Shit," I said, "I didn't know the fucking ducks were dirty," but eventually, when I got back to Liz, she'd stopped asking me for water and none of it mattered anyway.

XVIII

Meg's not here. I've got scratch burns up the inside of my thigh, probably from going over the fence, and bruises everywhere, probably from falling off it. I'm naked again, in bed, the sun's up. My clothes are a pile on the dresser, next to the coins from my pockets, one bill, a penknife, my handkerchief and tape measure. Shit, I'm practically skint. Nothing for it but to wait for Meg's return.

A maid enters, pushing a vacuum cleaner over the napless carpet.

"We're not checked out," I tell her.

"You only pay to Sunday night," she says. "You no here."

"I am now."

"Check out ten o'clock."

"My luggage is still here," pointing to the small, half-circle gym bag on a chair next to the dresser. She examines it.

"This you call luggage?"

I rise, sheets wrapped round like Caesar, take the bag from her. "We're not checked out."

Hands on her hips, head shaking: "Uh-uhhh. You no pay for Monday. You stay, you pay for Monday or your room rented someone else."

"You'll have to leave so I can get dressed. Then I'll go down and pay for another day." She retreats. I wedge the chair under the doorknob soon as she's gone, count the money on the dresser. Thirteen dollars and forty-three cents. The room's fifty bucks a night. I go back to bed.

"And quit swiping my pillow mints," I shout as an afterthought.

Thirteen bucks buys plenty of breakfast at The Onion, but that means leaving the room. Possession's nine-tenths and Meg wouldn't know where to find me. Smarter to hang, wait for her, make some phone calls while I'm waiting. Long distance. I charge them to the room.

"You are telling me this why?" Rajiit Singh is a decent guy for a Metro blue.

I'd called his home in Mississauga first, but he wasn't there. His wife expected him home soon. Something about a sick kid. Then I phoned my home.

Steve picked up.

"We might be staying a bit longer than planned," I told him.

"Okay."

"Everything all right?"

"Sure."

Another thought. "Heard from Meg?"

He hadn't.

It's another hour before I finally hear Rajiit's long vowels on the line. I've told him the story of Gretchen's two dads, plus the various and sundry acquaintances I've made this weekend, and he asks me why I called.

"You could pass on what I've told you, look good to your bosses." I add. "Then use your newly earned influence to get my car back. Or you could just tell me anything you know about these characters."

"The man you call Topcoat is Detective Sean Brogan. He does not like uniformed officers telling him his work."

"He's an asshole."

"Restraint is a virtue, John. You should remember that this asshole holds the keys to your car. Address him directly." There was a voice in the background calling Rajiit's name.

"Offer what you have discovered as a token of your esteem. Tell him what you told me, that you helped only to facilitate the return of your car. It will make him feel wise for taking it from you in the first place." The background voice again, a bit louder.

"I can't fault him on that. The chevy had to be impounded as evidence."

"That is the spirit."

"Except kissing-up might only encourage Brogan to hold the chevy longer, don't you think? He'll have a bottomless appetite for butt-licking, you want my opinion."

"You have only one other choice: buy another car, a good idea in any event. Dammit John, the payments on a small, new car would probably be less than what it costs you to put gas in that jitney anyway."

"Hey. The chevy's a classic. Someone told me that just the other day."

He hasn't heard. A hand came over the receiver to muffle the voices of domestic dispute. "Listen," he comes back on. "I must now go. I was to pick up Ariel's prescription on the way home from the doctor. Now Melba is too busy to fetch it because of washing and *Days of Our Lives*."

"A minute more Rajiit. Anything you hear about the victim, Toby. I'm told he worked at a laundry or diaper service."

He allows me to hear his sigh. "Yes. I knew there would be more."

He pauses for me to respond, but I hold out, making him fill the quiet.

"With you it is always something more. I know nothing of this man but you wish me to find out, asking questions that will bring me dangerously close to poking my nose into Brogan's affairs, something I have already told you I do not wish to do."

"Just some information," I say. "Whatever background you can find out. I'm not asking you to talk to Brogan directly."

"You don't think he has his flunkies? To get anything worth knowing I must eventually ask someone who will tell me little and quickly report my curiosity back to Brogan."

Fine, but I've got my own future as Meg's flunky to consider. "I wouldn't ask if it wasn't important, Rajiit."

He has to phone me back. "That is not such a good place you are staying, John," Rajiit says when I give him the hotel's address and phone number. "But you would know that already." Voices again in the background. "You should visit us some time for a holiday. Melba and I are both missing you, though perhaps not so much at the moment. I must go."

"I will. I've a friend I'd like you to meet," but the line has gone dead.

Meg still isn't back. Her book is on the night table. Her toothbrush, I can see, is still in the bathroom. Okay, she hasn't packed her luggage and run home.

I call her aunt's place. Ursula hasn't heard from Meg either.

"Vhy don't you come back here? I teach you the breaststroke." I can hear a motor running, and imagine her with a vacuum in one hand, phone in the other, cigarette dangling from her lips. Make that a small, black cigar.

"Sounds inviting, but I think I should find your boss first."

"She is not my boss. Not even her aunt is my boss. The two of them couldn't boss themselves vithout me to follow around and clean up after."

"Yeah well, it seems I may have lost her just the same."

"Oho, the great detective! Don't take it so hard. You are not the first," Ursula says.

"What's that supposed to mean?"

"A man has called every day. He said he vas Meg's close friend, they camp together. I tell him she's vith a big, strong ex-cop now, and so he stopped calling. I think, maybe there is more to you than I thought. But now you have called again and spoiled all my illusions."

Camp? What the fuck is camp? Somehow I can't see Meg rising early, tousle-haired from a damp sleeping bag to burn eggs over a Coleman stove. But I remember that for some people, camp means cottage.

I get Steve back on the line. "Anyone been calling, asking about me or Meg?"

"Yeah. Some guy said he was a friend of Mrs. Robinson, you know, the lady next door?"

The lady next door. I've shielded the boy. He doesn't know the half of it. "She hasn't been around has she?" I'm in the mood to blame Sue-Anne Robinson for my present circumstances. Anyone but me.

"What'd he want?"

"Who?"

"The guy who called?"

"Oh, he was looking for Meg. I told him you were both gone to Toronto, to the racetrack. Was that all right?"

"An off-track," I correct, "but yeah, that's more than all right. How'd you know?"

"You told me. In a note, with the twenty bucks you left for emergencies."

"Right. Spend it all?"

"Bought some eggs. Cereal."

"How'd he sound?"

"Who?"

"The guy who called."

"Oh. I don't know. Like a guy looking for someone I guess."

"Okay, don't worry about it. He didn't come around, did he?"

"No."

"Good. Listen, can you put next month's rent in an envelope and send it down here? It's the Beaches Hotel, Queen Street East. Wait, I'll get the address."

"It's on your note."

"Good. Go to that mailbox place and use a courier. That way I'll have it tomorrow. You can pay the fee from your rent."

"Um, well."

Shit. "Okay. Never mind. We'll sort it out when I get back. If I ever do." Better not mention this to Meg. She'll have me paying Steve for sitting house while we're gone.

I strip, go into the bathroom, run the tub taps until something more than rust comes out. The maid hasn't left any new bottlettes of shampoo or lotions for me. All I have is the sliver of soap left from yesterday. Careful not to drop it. Not enough room in here to bend over and pick it up.

It's taken a lifetime of practice, but I can scrub my ass, chew gum and think all at the same time. I try to sort what I know so far about Toby, Cartwright and the rest.

But all I come up with is what an asshole I am moping around the hotel room while Meg is out there alone, stirring up the low-life. I'm pulling my socks back on when the maid comes back banging on the door. Sounds like she's brought extra muscle this time. Meg's toothbrush, book, and yesterday's newspaper go into the gym bag along with my dirty underwear. Don't want our luggage seized for back rent. I remove the chair from the door. Two angry hotel employees fall into the room. One of them is the old Chinese guy I've seen across the road at The Farm, kissing up to Neville.

"I would not stay a moment longer in this room," I say, stepping over them, "even if you paid me."

XIX

Need some cash if I'm going to hang around town much longer. Jeezus, but hanging around town has started to look a lot like work. I ponder the possibilities over steak and eggs at The Onion.

What in hell should I do about Meg? Probably she's gone shopping or visiting Toronto friends I don't know about. Be nice if she'd told me, but I'm a grown man, able to entertain myself for awhile. Maybe she's pissed enough with me to blow town for some reason I don't know. Well she's old enough to look after herself. Worst thing, she might be investigating Toby's murder by herself. I know for sure I'm going to feel a right shit-heel if I go home while something nasty has happened to her here.

I don't feel good about selling Malcolm the chevy either, but don't see I've much choice. I look him up in the phone book, hop a bus hoping he won't notice I've failed to bring the merchandise with me. The upside of having the chevy in the City of Toronto's tender care is Malcolm won't see the damage done by Sherk. I open negotiations by offering the chevy as security for a loan.

"You want to borrow, see Neville," he says. Shit. I've already bought him a Coke from the machine standing outside his garage door. Not good to appear overeager if I want a good price. One of the selection buttons on the pop machine, I notice, is covered, "out of order" written on masking tape in black felt pen.

"Neville lends money?"

"That's his business. Get a hundred today, give him a hundred and a quarter next payday."

Christ, I'm getting past it. Seen Neville at The Farm dozens of times and only now realize I've never seen him place a bet. It's so obvious now. That's where he works. One place, anyway.

"What if there is no payday? I'm officially retired, you know."

"Pay the vigorish, you'll be all right."

"If I don't?"

"That's what Cecil's for, but I never actually seen it come to that, no sir. How much you looking for?"

"And? What happens then?"

He rubs at his grease-creased brow with the pop can. "Well now that depends. You own a business, then you got a new partner, fifty/fifty off the top. You don't own a business do you?"

Just a little hotel shakedown scam I might open in the Hammer someday, things work out Meg's way. "Crime fighter," I say.

"Or, you need a job, Neville will put you to work at one of his partnership places, salary comes out of his partner's half. It's been the start of many careers, borrowing money from Neville."

Everybody looking out for my employment prospects. "That how Toby got into the diaper business?"

"Can't say for sure. Probably. Those two guys working in the lube bay?" he points with the pop can, "Neville's boys, uh-huh. Give you two thousand for the chevy."

"Aren't you afraid he'll squeeze you out?"

"Felt nothing yet, nope. Fact is, if I skipped drawing salary and stiffed a few suppliers for the month, I could have paid Neville out. Only he's a good businessman. The Quickie Lube was his idea. Best move I've ever made, for sure. More than pays its way, and brings business into the repair bays. But the place still needs good, on-site management. That's what I do, and I take home more now than before Neville joined in. Everybody makes out."

There you go. Shylocks right after hookers in the heart-of-gold department. "You said half of ten for the chevy, last we talked."

He peers into the keyhole of the Coke can like it might hold a better number, grits his teeth and throws the nearly full pop in the garbage. "Should of taken it, uh-huh. Twenty-five, tops."

"Four-fifty, or I go find Neville."

"Suit yourself. He's on rounds Mondays, picking up," Malcolm checking a big clock on the wall inside, behind a desk stacked with grease-smudged papers. "Nearly lunch. He should be at the laundry, uh-huh, up on Dundas." Malcolm points to a riffled phone book. "York Laundry and Diaper Service, I think it is."

"Spot me ten for a cab?" He glares like I'm the stranger he wishes I was, sighs, makes the bell ring on his register. "Better make it twenty, in case I miss him," I say.

I borrow the use of his phone too, while Malcolm unlocks the Coke cooler, takes two beers from the column behind the "out of order" button. When I get back to him he's re-locking the machine.

"What happens if you gamble away the rest of the business?"

Head shake. "Neville won't lend me more'n a hundred, no sir," he says, heading inside, to the lunchroom I guess. "Sics Cecil on anyone who will. Did you know Neville was a doctor? The two of 'em ran some kind of clinic down in the islands, so they say. Take your nuts, one at a time, uh-huh, very clean. You don't miss more than a day's work, either. Not that I know anyone who's been under their scalpel."

"What is he, partners in a clinic? Should have had them do your vasectomy. Might have got half off," I tell Malcolm.

I admire Neville's enforcement technique in the cab back to the hotel. It's slick enough to put my visit to the laundry on hold. What else can you take that no man wants to give and still leave him with something more to lose? Taking one or both doesn't reduce the stiff's ability to repay, either, unless he's a star in the porno industry that flourishes sporadically in Toronto's west end.

Neville and Cecil can do it on the kitchen table with a local anaesthetic, a sharp scalpel, needle and thread. And the victim's cooperation. Gets messy without that, which is maybe why you'd want to cooperate.

"You have a choice. Lay back, relax, I'll give you something for the pain, or these boys will each take a leg while Cecil goes to work down there."

The knife work on Toby had been messy. Maybe he hadn't been given any options, or maybe the threat of losing one testicle didn't work on him. Apparently he didn't hold still. How often does a diaper truck driver get to use both nuts anyway?

So I put the idea of borrowing from Neville on hold. My plastic is maxed, and I've resisted getting one of those bank-machine cards. That way I still get to exchange insults with the overly-accessorized women and unwed mothers who cling to these bank wicket jobs. And that's as far as my thoughts take me. A pension cheque is due in my mail next week. Give Neville first dibs, I might get by fine. Be back bowling the home lanes in two weeks, tops. Not a time to be hasty.

Meanwhile, I'll check out the hotel and its environs, see if Meg's shown. It's stupid. She's the one run out on me. She's not helpless. If she isn't there, I'll run a sweep of our recent haunts.

"Has the lady returned to our room?" I ask the maid who has now taken up the post behind the lobby check-in counter at the Da-Nite.

"Lady?"

"The woman who shares my room."

She gives me a look says she doubts any woman sharing a room with me could be called a lady, but instead she says: "You lose her already?" The beginning of a grin working the corner of her lips.

Hell with it. My foot's on the first stair. Go up to the room, have a look for myself.

"Stop."

She's going to tell me nobody's up there, I know it, and that we've lost the room. Instead, the maid/receptionist offers a slip of white paper over the counter. "You have message. A policeman come for you. He want me to call him you come back."

She watches me return, take up the slip of paper, like five dollars might delay her call to the cops, ten bucks would stop it all together.

"Beaches Hotel" across the top of the chit. No name, no words, but I recognize Rajiit's cell number.

"I wouldn't worry about it," I tell her. "I'll call him myself."

✦ ✦ ✦

"Neville there?"

"Neville?"

I still wear the watch Liz gave me for our twenty-fifth anniversary. I've had it repaired twice. It would be cheaper to replace. Maybe I'm getting too attached to things. They don't bring people back, just memories. Can't trust memories. The watch lens is scarred, fuzzing some of the numbers, but I have no trouble telling time: just before one. I have to borrow from Neville, I'll need to catch him now. Midday, Malcolm had said.

I've already insisted, been passed up the line to manager at York

Laundry. "Is the owner in?" I try.

"I am the owner. Owner and manager. There's no one named Neville here."

At this point, men who expect better of themselves smack their foreheads. Neville's position at York Laundry and Diaper Service isn't on paper. He's a silent partner. Too silent right now.

Except Wally knew about it, and Malcolm. Malcolm didn't hide the fact that Neville had part of his business. What's different here?

"Listen, when he comes in, tell him John Swan called. A friend of his from out of town. Got some business I can throw his way."

How's he going to reach me? I've been tossed from the hotel, using the pay phone outside the liquor store where I found Squeegee Boy the other night. Before I can come up with a plan, there's footsteps on the line, the sound of an office door closing. Footsteps coming back. If I wanted my shirts done, I'd have hung up and tried someplace else by now. Sound of a hand over the receiver. Voice comes back, low.

"I don't know who you are, but there's no Neville here. If you don't stop calling and bothering my staff, I'll be forced to notify your superiors."

I've only called the Laundry this once. Someone else is looking for Neville, someone who knows he's usually at the Laundry on Mondays. Apparently they've been persistent.

"Who you think's been calling you? Cops?"

The sound of air pushed from the back of the throat, no word, a guttural "as if" sound before the line starts to buzz.

✦ ✦ ✦

"Listen, this is what I have to tell you." Rajiit says. "I have gotten nothing about this Neville, but the man Toby's death has put a live-wire up bottoms in several east-end divisions. Diapers were only part of your victim's trip. The rest was linen service to small restaurants and taverns."

I've called Rajiit from the pay phone, right after finding I was out of quarters, hitting up the hotel desk clerk for change. Jeez she's got a foul way about her.

"Neville's also a shy, I found out since we talked this morning. He owns part of the Laundry, though you won't find that registered on any deed."

"This makes sense. Many of this Toby's stops were establishments frequented by known bookmakers," Rajiit adds.

"So Toby's a runner?"

"No one has stuck their nose into a diaper pail to bring up hard evidence, but laundry bags would make a good way to move slips and cash. I have spoken only to an east-end patrolman. Melba and I bowl with him and his wife Doris Tuesday nights. He says the victim was quickly recognized at the daily briefing. Many knew the truck. The laundry is a known front for gambling."

"But not Neville's connection to it," I finish.

"No. That I have learned from you."

"Lotteries and casinos were supposed to put illegal gambling out of business by now."

"Sure. That has skimmed some action at the same time it has whet new appetites. There is no legal sport book in Canada. If you have played the lottery pools, you know they are a poor substitute. The Internet has eaten into street bookmaking, but many still do not own computers. Some prefer to deal in money matters the old way, face to face."

Exactly the way I feel about my bank tellers.

"Neville's bookmaking supports his shylocking. The shylocking has taken him into other businesses."

"But the scene is fluid," Rajiit continues. "There is very little customer loyalty anymore. Loan sharking takes up the action. Whether they lose legal or illegal, bettors still borrow. If your Neville is a shylock involved in gaming, it is almost quaint."

"I've seen him around The Farm for years and never put it together. If I had to guess, I'd say he was a shy first, and that got him into organized bookmaking. I could be wrong, but Jesus, you can't run an independent book in this city can you?"

"Not since your Johnny Pops had his talk with Max Bluestein forty years ago. There is territory poaching though, and new, ethnic gangs who grow dissatisfied preying only on their own communities. The situation is very volatile."

"Could Toby be the first shot in a turf war?"

"Possibly so. Look, I must go now. I have promised to watch Rodney play soccer this afternoon and I am already ten minutes late. As I said, I did not get anything about this Neville, or Cecil. You are the only one who has connected them with the York Laundry."

"I didn't make it up, Rajiit."

His voice changes, the pitch rising. "I don't doubt you. I am only saying the constable I spoke with has not heard these names. I must be going now, please. Here is what I am wanting to tell you. If you tell Brogan about these two characters, he might go easy on you and your car. Goodbye."

"If it hasn't been torn apart already."

I decide it can't hurt to take Rajiit's advice and share with Brogan. A few beeps and clicks and I've got someone who knows someone who might have met Brogan at the policemen's ball if I'll tell them the purpose of my call.

"My name's Swan. Brogan's got a murder case, happened in the parking lot of the Beaches Hotel on Queen East. I have some information may help."

"One moment please."

Whoever invented elevator music should spend a lifetime on hold on the police line. Has to be the reason everyone dials 911 even when there is no emergency. I learn five steps to streetproof children, including the all-important: "Policemen are your friends." Then I'm given a ten-point road-safety check so my car won't be impounded next time I'm arbitrarily stopped by the blue boys. Finally listed are the countless reasons why the city should buy helicopters for cops at something like three million a pop. I'm close to debating with the recording when an only slightly more human voice comes back on the line.

"Okay, I can write this down and have Brogan call you when he gets in. Your name again please?"

"Swan. Tell him..." Christ, there's too much to just leave a message. Besides, I'd like to get some info in exchange. Like whether Gretchen's been found, or if Brogan knows about her weekend hangout or the stepdad's part in the kid's drug buys. And I don't have a number any more where he can call me back. If he calls the hotel, he'll think I've skipped and get curious why. Shit.

"Tell him I'll call back."

XX

It's past time to start looking for Meg. I run a quick tour of our recent haunts starting with a window check at the liquor store, because, after the pizza joint, it's the first place outside the hotel. Next, the joints between here and The Beaches.

The Farm is closed Mondays. I stand at the corner entrance to Olde Woodbine Estates, wondering if Meg would go in there alone, and why. Across the road a secretary watches me from the window of the model home sales office. She picks up the phone from her desk, punches buttons below my line of sight. Down the street a car engine starts. I see the security company cruiser shift away from the curb and its roof lights start to twirl. I'll leave this for later, when the gate-keeper's gone home. Meg's not in the bookstore, further east. She's not in the sex emporium. I could go in and ask the sales clerk if Meg's been in, but think how I'll look chasing after a woman in a room full of plastic cocks? They've probably got 911 on speed dial in there.

I check the library on a whim, go through Kew Park to the beach. Nothing. The shore's noisy, waves building on fall winds. The way back is uphill, softball diamonds in a pit dug into the slope. This place used to produce sports heroes to spread over the city and the country. Means shit to nobody now but the occasional fart limping on plastic knees, or odd biddies collecting cat fur between pages of their local history books.

Meg's not in the restaurant where we ate Friday. No, that was Saturday. She's not in the pub where I waited for her to finish her shopping. Further along is another park, smaller, cut at an angle into a side street. Dark and leafy, Meg could be stuffed behind some shrub while I'm thinking she's on the wander. Big city. A million places she could be, or could be dumped if she's come to harm. Back to the pub, order a Smithwicks while I warm. Meg's someone takes care of herself. Strange to think of her as victim, but it happens. She said last night: "That's what gets girls dumped." Something like that.

What can I do? It's not like I'm on friendly terms with the cops. I could report it through Rajiit, but even he'll tell me to wait. She's been gone only a few hours. I've only known her a few days. They'll figure she's run off with some guy. Hell, I think so too, mostly.

On the TV behind the bar cops move through the Beaches Hotel parking lot. "Still unsolved" a newscast twist says. Toby's murder. She flashes a long dimple up one cheek as she reads from the teleprompter. Pic of Toby alive and clean-shaven. I wouldn't recognize him without the voice-over. I could watch the dimple on that twist come and go all day. Pic of the ex-wife being comforted by the new hubby. I recognize him. "Missing since Friday," the newscaster continues, "is young Gretchen, the Cartwright's thirteen-year-old daughter." Not quite getting it right but answering one of the questions I had for Brogan.

The husband in the newscast is Cartwright, the man I saw Neville meet over mussels and white wine the last time I was in this joint, waiting for Meg to buy underwear. He fits the description Doggo the Squeegee Boy gave me. He'd been straight about that, at least. It takes a fistful of fingers to count the people who'd benefit from the diaperman's death, including Doggo himself if Toby had started to figure the Squeegee Boy's connection to Gretchen. Cartwright would benefit the same way, not to mention ridding himself of the nuisance Toby was causing with custody lawsuits. Count the ex-wife and her old man, O'Keefe, in on that. They'd suffer any taint to the Olde Woodbine Estates development. But O'Keefe and the Cartwrights are experienced and successful manipulators. Born to it. They might be behind Toby's death, but they'd keep their thumbs out of the gutting itself.

Now the kid, Gretchen, she hadn't exactly applauded the opportunity to give up her weekends for more quality time with the original bio-dad. Then again, she had no trouble ditching him when she felt the need to hangout with her drug buddies. What if Toby tracked her down, confronted her? Never know what'll come of these parent/teen standoffs. Kids today are so impulsive.

A young couple coos at the table where Neville and Cartwright broke bread last Saturday. Neville and Cartwright make unlikely bedfellows, but Wally mentioned Toby as a link between the two. Cartwright's wife was Toby's ex. They were both Gretchen's father. And Toby worked for Neville.

Logic says follow the money. Toby needed money to finance custody suits against his ex-wife. What bank would loan thousands to a diaper delivery-man with a history of breakdown and addiction? How many friends could Toby have who could lend him thousands and wait forever to be repaid? What did Toby have for collateral? Neville had the money, but shylocks are generally less patient than banks when it comes to collection time. What would Neville get out of helping Toby? The link to Cartwright, maybe. Leverage. Neville could have used Toby's legal maneuvers for the custody of Gretchen to show he could interrupt at will, the care and feeding of the real-estate tycoon's cronies.

Toby didn't seem much like father material when I met him, but all Neville would have to do is clean him up for a few court appearances and let some high-priced lawyer do the talking. To make this worthwhile, would Neville have to know about Gretchen's weekends in the city, muling for Cartwright? No. That information was more dangerous to Cartwright than any law suits. Neville wouldn't have had to bother with the legal work if he'd known about that. But if Neville had found out about Gretchen's doings in the process of suing Cartwright, Toby himself would have no further purpose. He might even have become a liability, a loose, open-mouthed cannon.

Everyone with a good reason to kill Toby has good reasons to leave him be, work around him. That's what comes of following the money when all the players have it and want more.

Things are usually simple as they look. Toby is probably the first salvo in a bookmakers' turf war. One of Neville's competitors horning in, as Rajiit and I speculated. Toby had been killed with a knife. I'd come up against a couple of them this weekend myself. Too many knives, too many people wanting Toby dead for him to live past Saturday.

But Toby will keep. What I should be doing now is finding Meg. I pay the barkeep, start the long walk back to Java Hut and The Onion. I've been there already today, but there's nothing for it but to go round the circuit again, and again if I have to, checking cafés and shop windows along the way until I find her. It's lousy beat-cop work, what makes donut shops look inviting. I cover two of them before passing the hotel and the liquor store again.

Further along, the big shouldered man with black brows stands dead centre in the square cinder-box that is the Italian café. Son of a bitch scans the traffic outside his place like he's some sort of mobbed-up Neighbourhood Watch.

I've a sudden urge to go inside, stretch the counter debit machine to the end of its coiled cord and smash it into the man's face. Not because there's any proof he's mobbed up, but because he's so stupid he's put his family's savings into this small-business fantasy, dreams of earning enough to buy a delivery shit-box while he drives his bambinos to Sunday Mass in a Buick smelling of pepperoni grease and anchovies. Such smiling faith in the honest buck begs to get split by a piece of cutting-edge technology hard-wired to a bank computer.

Two rag-asses at the streetcar turn-round, sucking lonely teeth, agree to have seen anybody I want for a loonie. Middle-aged boys flip coins on the corner at Coxwell. They seen no Meg, man, but can hook me up with a bitch blond to her pussy hairs I can call her any name I want.

Fifty-three Division is only two blocks north. Will they know anything about Meg there, or at a hospital? Too early to risk the visit. I look in on The Onion, then take the other side of Queen going east, expecting less with each step, plan to check out Gretchen's stomping grounds again this circut.

And suddenly there's Cecil.

✦　✦　✦

Three of them in the theatre coffee shop behind a rolling glass garage-door that opens to summer weather. I backtrack, duck into the chrome lobby. It was Cecil caught my eye. I'd have gone by but for him.

"Where's Neville?" I ask. Cecil shaking his head as I realize Meg has one of the seats across the table.

"You might have woke me up," I tell her.

"You looked so comfortable, darling, I thought I'd let you sleep in." Eyelids aflutter.

"I've been looking for you all day."

"That wasn't necessary. You should have waited in the room."

"We've been tossed from the room."

"No we have not. I paid for another night this morning, after I went back to the hotel and discovered you'd abandoned me."

"I didn't abandon you. You were already gone when I woke up."

Cecil's eyes are hooded, but he has that smile again, broad enough to light the lobby.

She puts down her tea and gives me a once-over. "You spent the whole night talking about your wife. Do you miss her so much?"

"Of course I miss her. We can talk about this later. Come on."

"You wish she were here instead of me." Her back is rigid, not touching her chair.

I shake my head. "No."

"Then why would you talk about her in your sleep?"

Cecil looks around to see who else is getting this.

"I told you he was wrong for you Meg."

"Shut up Stan," I say, paying attention finally to the third person at the table, the one that fills the seat next to Meg. Stan Walters, of the lets-go-to-the-cottage-and-fuck-our-friends Walters. He's tracked Meg faster than I have. I left way too much information in my note to Steve.

"It's not a competition, Meg. Liz is gone. I mean, Jesus, can't we talk about this some other time?"

"Don't you think that's even more humiliating, making me compete with a dead person?"

Stan waved his arm toward the window, and Queen Street beyond. "I've come to deliver Meg from this squalidity."

Squalidity? "Shut the fuck up Stan. You want me to phone Marcie and tell her what you're doing here?"

There's a near empty cup of tea on the table before Meg, a full cup of coffee in front of Cecil. Stan has been working on a paper boat of nacho chips smothered in orange glop.

"I've left Marcie," he says.

"Then you're a bigger asshole than I took you for."

"No, Stan," Meg says, like it's a tragedy. A smile, quickly covered.

"It had to come, Meg. Marcie and I talked it all out. Once I showed her how things were she agreed to step aside to let me find the happiness I'm destined to share with you." Meg's competition for affection may be a dead person, but suddenly I envied her.

"You want to be careful man, make sure you destiny isn't through Cecil."

Here's the thing. Neville's not around, and there are other signs Cecil's off the leash. He's changed his style. His cap is gone, his hair in cornrows, and the three-quarter-length black leather coat he's wearing is shiny new. It's open. Cecil sits up, slides his right hand into the coat pocket as he speaks. If experience is a teacher, I know what that means. Cecil has moved up a step in the world of the squalidity that has Stan's shorts in a twist. I know Stan meant me, but when it comes to squalidity, I'm willing to share.

"Aren't you boys a bit confused? Meg darling, what have you been doing all day to get these fags so fucked up?"

"What's that supposed to mean?" Stan says.

"I did some shopping, as you can see," Meg says. She turns this way and that, so we can each admire her new sweater and her bust-line in the best light. "Then I thought I might meet you at The Farm, but it's closed Mondays, so I had lunch and shopped some more." A big plastic bag rests at her ankles. "I went back to the hotel a number of times, but you weren't there. That's where Stan found me. Then we went out and later we ran into Cecil. So I suggested we all see a movie."

"Hey I'm talking to you Mr. Big-time Ex-cop. What did you mean by that comment?" Stan again.

"Means I don't understand why you're bothering Meg when Cecil's the bumboy."

He splutters. "What?"

"Oh come on. It's a whole new millennium. Step out of the closet. Meg told me about you and Ham down at the cottage dock." I make a circle with the thumb and finger of my left hand, and penetrate it with the forefinger of my right. "How was it, by the way?"

"What?" he spits again, orange drool spraying the tabletop.

"The movie."

"It was okay," Meg answers. "I don't think the boys liked it very much, but they're just too polite to say so." She looks from one to the next, to see how they take to being called "boys." "What have you been up to John?" she asks when there's no response from them.

Stan stands. "You filthy bastard."

"Already told you, I've been looking for you, and trying to figure what happened to Toby, like you asked."

"What did you find?"

Stan kicks over his chair for emphasis. "I said 'you filthy bastard.'" Gets attention from the girl hustling behind the coffee counter. Decor here is all silver and dark wood tones. I'm an orange Formica man myself.

"The usual. Everyone is more than they appear. Take Cecil here. He's Neville's bumboy as I said. Only where's Neville today?" I ask.

Cecil shrugs, faces Meg. "You want to know about Neville, go ask Neville."

All my visits to The Farm I've never seen Cecil but there's Neville close by. This is the second time this weekend I've spotted Cecil on his own and I haven't been able to find Neville where I was told he can usually be found every Monday. "I have business for him," I say.

"Nobody calls me queer. Let's step outside," Stan's bunched up in a thick wool sweater-jacket with black and yellow trim. I picture Marcie knitting it for him twenty years ago to wear to his Saturday football games. A Tiger-Cat leaps across the right breast pocket. Marcie should have saved herself the effort.

"This is what happens when you run your act before dickheads too dumb to know you're only playing," I tell Meg.

"That's it. You and me, pal, outside. Now." Stan.

Meg asks. "Who says I'm playing?"

"I do."

I smoosh the cheesy gondola into Stan's face, hooking my heel behind his so he goes down into the mess of empty chairs behind him.

Cecil laughs, looks around at the attention we've drawn from staff and loitering movie buffs. "Leave these two children," he says to Meg. "You and me finish what we started Friday night, huh?"

I take Meg's arm. "You shouldn't lead people on. How's anybody going to know when you mean it?"

She shakes free. "I mean what I say I mean. You think you can talk about your ex-wife all night long and then just come in here and order me around?"

That again. Christ. Staff have come to help Stan up. Cecil has his smile back. He still has his right hand in his coat pocket. I thought at first what he had in it was intended for Stan, but now I think maybe the blade's been waiting for me all along.

"If this is what you want," I tell her, "he's all yours."

XXI

"Don't think you can go back to the hotel either," she shouts to my back. "That's my room. I paid the rent, remember?"

Standing on the sidewalk in Splitsville is grim with only change in your pocket. No kip. No car. Not even the cash for the bus ride home. Dramatic exits are long on feel-good but short on what-now.

I won't have Meg see me hesitate, so I stride east along Queen. Only last night I sang naked on a rooftop. Tonight my ass is hanging out again.

"Need a lift Swanee?"

It's a limo, black. Not a stretch. Front window's rolled down, Wally's face dripping out. "Somebody like to talk to you," he says, tilting his head toward the back seat.

I bend low to look in. The glass is tinted.

"It's okay," Wally says. "He don't bite."

The rear door releases. I pull it back. There's an old man sprawled in the far corner. His hair is silver, extends over the collar of his blue chenille shirt. One long arm extends across the seat back, ending in deeply tanned, manicured fingertips. The other holds a cut-glass tumbler filled more than half by golden liquid. Tan slacks touch the ample floor space, the leather soles on his shoes as soft and thin as slippers. He's rich and comfortable with it. Reminds me again of the man I saw on Meg's arm the night of her aunt's fundraiser.

"This is the man I told you about, Mr. O'Keefe," Wally says.

"Thank you Wally. Anthony will take care of you," O'Keefe says.

Wally takes an envelope from the chauffeur, gets out, holds the rear door for me.

"A drink Mr. Swan?"

"That doesn't look like Heaven Heather," I say.

O'Keefe smiles. "Oh, I think you'll find it agreeable enough."

I get in. The car pulls from the curb. The lock buttons descend into the rear doors.

"Wally tells me you've taken an interest in my affairs."

It makes me laugh, Wally outside The Farm yesterday eagerly telling me all he knew about Toby and O'Keefe, then running off to O'Keefe to get a reward for telling him there was a detective snooping around.

O'Keefe stops pouring. "Did I say something funny?"

The car turns right toward the lake.

"No," I say.

He straightens the decanter, hands me the glass. "I'm an old man, Mr. Swan. Lived long enough to know the world is filled with evil and confusion. I expect I may have contributed to that in my younger days. Now I want to make that right. I've dedicated myself to bringing order to the world. As much as one man can. This little corner at least." He extends his arm toward my window, the Olde Woodbine Estates passing outside. "For instance, with this project I've transformed the risk and chaos of the racetrack to the order and security of a modern housing development. Every measure has been designed, every household feature built so that Olde Woodbine is a place where families will feel safe and comfortable planning their lives, raising their children."

"Gee, thanks."

He laughs. "No, Mr. Swan, I don't expect any public appreciation for what I do. It's enough to do my share and avoid the confusion of evil that still exists in this world. Do you understand what I'm saying Mr. Swan?"

"Not exactly." I hand him my empty glass. "Try again, a little slower."

The car turns left off Lakeshore Road and stops beside a stretch of grass leading down to the beach.

"Do you golf, Mr. Swan?"

"Not if I can help it."

He puts my glass back into the little cabinet he took it from. I miss it already. "Come on. We'll drive a few."

The trunk lid pops as we get out the car. Inside is a golf bag and a bucket of dimpled balls. "Do you mind carrying the bag for me? Anthony has to stay with the car. You never know the sort of people to be found around here at night. An untended automobile could be a target."

We walk about twenty yards down the grass. It's dark, cool and empty. O'Keefe stops and takes a ball from the bucket, sets it up on a tee from his pocket about three inches from my big toe. He selects a wood from the golf bag.

"What can you tell me about my granddaughter and my son-in-law?" he asks. The club arcs and whacks the ball out over the beach into the water.

"Who, Toby?"

He sets up another ball. "Yes, that might be useful too, but I'm thinking about the second one, Morgan."

"Cartwright?"

He whacks the second ball toward the lake, looks at me and nods.

He's setting up the third ball. I drop the golf bag from my shoulder, feel around my pockets.

"Do you have a cigarette?" I ask.

"I'll have Anthony give you one when we get back to the car. Answer my question please."

"Cartwright and Gretchen? I don't know much. Nothing I could state as fact. Not a comfortable, orderly relationship, I'd say that."

He whacks the ball, sets up another. "Could you find out more?"

"Maybe. For the right price."

"If you found out something, would you tell me before you told the police?" Leaning on the club.

"Maybe."

He puts the club back in the bag, unzips a pocket and brings out a cheque book and pen.

"I'm told you were once a police officer. A detective in fact. I could hire you to do some detecting on my behalf?"

"You might."

"Would thirty thousand buy some discretion as well?"

"Fifty would buy more."

He laughs. "Yes, I'm sure it would. Why don't we start with thirty and see how things progress? Do you know where my granddaughter is?"

I shake my head. "She's been sleeping in your vacant finished houses..."

"Don't waste your time there. I have that under observation." He hands me the cheque. Looks good. Thirty grand, dated today, signed in the right place.

"Your rent-a-cop? I wouldn't count on him."

"Yes, I've seen the videotapes of your encounter. He's been reprimanded, I assure you."

"You've got the survey under video surveillance, you must have seen what she's been up to."

"Just enough to be worried. It's a parent's place to worry, Mr. Swan. I need to know the details. And I need to keep them safe with me." He picks up the golf bag. "Can I drop you somewhere?"

"Someplace I can get this cashed."

"Yes, I'm sorry I don't carry cash in that volume. It's not safe. Officially you're a security consultant for Olde Woodbine Estates."

"How much do you carry? A C-note would be handy right now."

He smiles and nods. "Any bank will cash that cheque tomorrow morning."

He walks back to the car and leaves.

I fold the cheque and put it in my pocket. I'm cash poor, no place to tender the cheque tonight and no place to sleep. I could tell Meg we've scored but she didn't want my company. Across Lakeshore is the back way into Olde Woodbine Estates. What the hell. I'm on the payroll, they can put me up for the night.

XXII

Down a few dusty, mud-chunked streets, round a bend of half-built houses searching for completed units yet to be inhabited. Good enough for Gretchen, good enough for me. Find one with the heat on, I'm golden.

There are fewer vacant houses than I expected. Market must be good. Do they sell them as they build them or build them as they sell them? Completed units have lights on, cars in the drive. Only a handful between them and the windowless shells. The few that fit between have deadbolts. Can't use my plastic to get by them. I should have asked Gretchen's grandad for a key.

I circle a couple of houses to find the easiest way in. Come morning I'll hitch home to the Hammer. That'll show Meg. Hell, I can phone Rajiit, probably get a ride. I could probably do it now, only I'm tired and not handy to a pay phone. I won't disturb Rajiit tonight. I'll be fine till morning. If not Rajiit, then somebody. Meg will show when she's done whatever she's doing. Probably flirting with someone she thinks will be better than me for her shakedown scams. Someone like Cecil maybe, who it turns out swings both ways, but doesn't already have thirty grand in his wallet. Shows what Meg knows.

No televisions or radios in the vacant units. Gretchen skipped The Farm ahead of Toby. It's possible she hasn't even heard of his death yet, but not bloody likely. Somebody would tell her. She can't have spent all weekend alone in a vacant house. Someone would come for her. If she was here, O'Keefe's confident she isn't now. He wants to find her before the cops.

Broken glass around the catch on a basement window. A careless workman or one of the kids. My only other choice is a unit closer to the occupied houses, where I might be heard breaking in. There might be somebody inside this one already. What are they going to say? Find your own place?

The opening is below grade, in a window well. I step down, push the window in and withdraw my hand. Nothing to hold the window open, but it's still an easy in. For a kid. Snug for a fifty-year-old fat man. If I smash one of the big glass patio doors around back I could walk right in, but that'd make noise and might be noticed when the sun comes up tomorrow morning. Who knows, I may want to sleep in. A big glass door open with the wind blowing in from the lake, the house would soon be as cool inside as out. There's a lot of thought required when you rough it on the streets. I give the basement window a try.

My wallet catches on the window frame. I climb out again, take off my pants, my jacket, roll them in a ball and throw them through the window ahead of me. A little strategic breath control and I'm in. A five-foot drop to the concrete floor. Can't see a damned thing beyond the light beam from the window. As I wait for my eyes to adjust I consider it could be the same house where I tried pitching woo with Meg Friday night. Can't see to find my coat and pants on the floor.

Feel my way along the wall, sweeping the poured concrete foundation with my arm. Hollow thunk of a metal box. The furnace. Feel along and around it. A noise. Close. Rustling. Concrete again. Around the plastic sewer pipe cemented into the floor and then wood. Steps. From behind. Around that, and still sweeping my arm along the wall in the dark until I find the metal box of a light switch. I have to chance it. Can't leave pants with my identification lying on the basement floor of a house I've just broken into. A moment for the glare to stop burning my eyes.

Smears of paint on the drywall leading up the stairway, a streak of rust-brown. Kids vandalizing the unit with leftover paint they've found, ketchup squeezed from a plastic pouch, maybe a workman cut by a sharp tool. Or something. I've left fingerprints all along the wall to the light switch.

There's more blood on the floor by the furnace, shoeprints tracking through. I lift one foot, twist. The shoeprints match the pattern on my sole.

Drag-streaks in the dust squeeze into the narrow space between furnace and wall. Desperate shuffling.

Blood, congealing, and movement under a pile of clothes wedged behind the furnace. I squeeze in to understand, extend my hand to pull away the top layer, leaning close when a face emerges. My head thunders against a hollow duct, as I jump from pairs of beady eyes pouring from under the blood-soaked coat. Rats. They had a good home when horseshit and feed filled the old racetrack stables. Now, with that gone, they take what comes their way.

Tonight they've got a bonus. A bloody body inside the clothing. Clothing I've seen before.

The head is turned to the wall deep in the far corner darkness. I back out, go around to the other corner for a look at the top of the body, the light a bit better from this angle. Not quite good enough. Flesh on the cheek bone going green. Rigor fading. I won't get a look at the face without pulling the body out. I'm not going to do that.

Something, a package, under the neck and shoulder. I need a reach, spot a yard of electric cable coiled by the roughed-in fireplace. It might be long and thick enough for the job. I bend the end into a hook and reach down the side of the furnace, catch a handle of printed cardboard and carefully tug. Rats move on the bits of flat-tened fried dough pulled from under the body's weight. A logo on the carton visible between their scurry. It says Java Hut, where Meg and I bribed Squeegee Boy, Doggo, for information. Now I know where I've seen that sweater. Someone's punched Doggo up since I did. I'm going to have to prove that.

Down to the window for my own coat and pants. I've left too much of me on the basement floor and walls to hide my presence. Blood caked into the treads of my shoes. Any forensics lab will easily match the distinctive nicks and wear patterns worked into the soles and heels of my footwear to the red footprints that start at the furnace and fade behind the cellar steps.

Then there's the fingerprints. I've probably even left fibre frag-ments of my shorts climbing through the window. Staff at Java Hut saw me talking to Doggo about Toby. Brogan's an asshole, not an idiot; he'll match two with two. I need an alibi. Where was I about twenty hours ago? Flying through the air and landing naked on a cop on Cherry Street. Shit shit shit.

I'm in it good. Running will only look worse. On with my coat and pants. Upstairs to call the cops. An empty coil of thin wires on the kitchen wall where someday a phone will be. The sales office, or a phone booth on Queen Street. No. One of the neighbouring, occupied houses. They're closer. My hand on the knob when the front door opens in on me, cracks me on the nose. It's broken, I fucking heard it crack, felt the shock to my ears. There's stars, a body rushing in with the door like a halfback as I go down; he scrapes across my face with his flashlight. It's the fucking survey rent-a-cop.

My luck is holding.

If only some of it was good.

✦ ✦ ✦

A long night of sirens, flashing lights, cruisers and yellow tape leads to this airless room in 55 Division like a streetcar rail from my first step into this trip.

Shirt and tie, bordered by the beige of a familiar trench coat. I have to look up to see Brogan's face. Concrete wall behind him, not institution green, not painted at all. I'm cuffed, my arms stretched out front, holding me half across a desk or table, the surface rough against my cheek. It's not steel or plastic. It's plywood. I hear voices. There are a pair of blues on a set of steps. A small pile of construction rubble at the bottom to one side. I'm not at 55 Division. I'm in another basement in the Olde Woodbine survey.

I thrash, rattle the chains, the plywood rocks precariously.

"Careful sunshine. You'll do yourself a tumble," Brogan says.

I feel a hand from behind, on my back, steadying. Brogan has something in his hands, a piece of paper.

"What's this about?" holding it before my eyes.

It's the cheque O'Keefe gave me. "Retainer. I'm the curity con-thultant for Olde Woodbine," my jaw stiff, my nose thick.

Brogan laughs. "What's that? Didn't quite get that."

Fuck him.

"Going private are you? Got your license, have you? Didn't see that in your wallet." He takes my wallet up from the table, makes a show of looking.

I shouldn't need a license to consult on security. Just to investigate. Would be better though. The thought comes, stupidly, if O'Keefe wants me quiet, he should hire me through his lawyer for confidentiality. Then I'd need a license. Have to talk to him about that before cashing the cheque.

"Hafta put that on my To Do Litht," I tell Brogan.

"Ha ha. Ever the comic, eh?" Brogan says. "Take my advice, stick with the stand-up. Leave the detective work to someone knows how."

And I realize, as the dry-gloved finger enters, why I'm not at 55. No video camera to record interrogation. Two cops stationed on the steps to keep out the curious. My legs spread, my pants and shorts at my ankles. Brogan in charge.

A cavity search goes easier if you cooperate. Write that down for when your turn comes. All I have for Brogan is gas. I'd have given it him anyway, but that's not what he wants. He's after giving it out.

"I know," he says as I bite down. "It's not pleasant is it? I wouldn't even let my doctor do that to me. It can go hard, or harder," there's a shove with each of the two words, "depending how I want it to go."

A comfortable sit-down, a week of the bloody shits, or an accidental rip and putrid infection: it's all up to Brogan and the blue with his fingers up my ass.

My impulse is to smile, laugh, show indifference, but I've lost control of facial expression.

"You're in my space now, Swan. After I'm done here I'll arrest you and have you in reach whenever I want you."

Another push and pain that buckles my knees. That's not fingers. That's a baton.

"You've got as much say about it as Constable Jerry Evans. You remember Constable Evans, don't you, the officer you jumped on Saturday night?"

"Nah mhe," I say through my blood-stuffed nose.

"Oh that was you all right. I can bring up ten officers who will identify you asking after a young girl at that warehouse, and probably twice as many kids who saw you dancing naked up on the roof." He's proud of this next bit: "I've even got a recorded 911 call about a man running naked across Lakeshore Road and dragging a woman behind the bushes. How many fat, naked, old men do you think run the streets of Toronto any given night?"

Chuckles from the stairs. The baton thrusts, waggles.

"He required hospitalization you know. Constable Evans. Two broken fingers on his left hand, bruised ribs, sprained ankle."

A pause in his monologue. I brace for another thrust. Instead the truncheon slips from between my legs. I let myself hope it's done.

"Not to mention the counselling Evans will need for the trauma he's suffered."

The laughter from the stairs increases, joined by snickering from behind me.

"The sight of your asshole descending on him from the heavens, big enough to swallow him whole."

Something smaller up me now, softer. Lubricated. It strokes, gently, a place I didn't know I had.

"It goes hard or it goes easy," Brogan continues. "All depends how I say it goes. You understand?"

I can't stop it, my knees knock. Not even hard, but I squirt onto the table.

"Enjoy a good fisting do you? Thought so," Brogan says. "Fucking pervert."

"Thorry," I say. "Thoughd you thwallowed."

He slaps my face into the plywood. "Clean that up," he says, pointing to my stain, but he doesn't say with what, or how. Both my hands are cuffed.

I shake my head. "I lefd early. Witneth." There were no cars on Lakeshore close enough to give a good description, and few kids out on the roof sober enough to testify. Sure I asked the extra-duty cops about Gretchen but that was an hour, at least, before the ladder incident. The only thing the cop I landed on can identify is my hairy ass and I doubt he can pick that out in a lineup. I don't have to be thinking clearly to know a good lawyer can walk me on this, especially if Meg says I was in bed with her, back at the hotel, at the time.

Means I'll have to make it up with Meg. Not for the first time I miss my brother Artie, the lawyer.

I may be muddled, but I can come up with the magic word: "Lawyer."

"Oh you don't need a lawyer yet. You're not under arrest, you're still in the process of resisting. And when you are in custody, it won't be for Constable Evans. I've got something much better. I've got you for the murder of Vince Donatelli, aka Vinnie the Dog or, as you undoubtedly know him: Doggo. Part-time squeegee entrepreneur, part-time drug pusher, part-time pimp, full-time sleaze."

Brogan smacks at my already broken nose. He'll lay his bruises off on the Olde Woodbine rent-a-cop, son of a bitch, flailing at me with his fucking flashlight when I tried to get out of the house. Prick probably doesn't even know yet I'm practically his boss.

I keep shouting "Lawyer!"

I remember a voice barking down at the two cops on the steps, followed by hushed whispers. I remember forms, ink on my fingers. I remember a cell, time washing down the drain in a concrete floor. I remember a man shining a small light, looking into my eyes.

It's dark when they wake me. Could be dark again. Could be dark still. I get my shoelaces back, my belt, and my little, half-moon gym bag. They show me some form I signed waiving medical attention. Christ I was obliging. They're letting me out. My Timex is broken. Never wear a good watch to a police interrogation. Miss Meyers, my grade one teacher, never said a thing about that. Another form to reclaim my chevy says I'm responsible for daily impound fees. That goes in the gym bag with the other paper work.

I expect to see Rajiit waiting on a bench when I drag-ass out to the lobby. Who else would hear I've finally made it to Division 55? Who else could pull favours, get me out? But it's not him.

It's Neville.

XXIII

"You look like shit," Neville says.

"You haf a low obinion of thit," I answer. I want to ask how he sprung me. "How?" is all I manage.

His hands lift, palms up. He shakes his head. "They scooped up Toby's daughter, Gretchen, with her boyfriend on the highway up by Barrie. Thumbing to Vancouver. The boyfriend, what's his name—Jason, confessed to killing Toby and Doggo."

He's in a shiny navy tracksuit and white runners, just another guy out for a jog except it's the middle of an endless night and he's collected his dreads in a rainbow wool beanie.

I shake off the idea. Doesn't hurt. Not much. "Wathn'd him," I say.

"Let's get out of here." He guides me through the door, leads south on Coxwell.

"Dime is id?"

"Morning soon enough."

"Kid'th nod the one."

"That doesn't matter. He's confessed. Got himself a high-priced lawyer and martyred himself for the girl Gretchen."

My knee buckles and I clutch at Neville for support. "Fucking athhole Brogan."

Neville's hand on my near elbow. "He makes his way, like anybody else."

It hurts to walk. I pull on Neville to stop a moment.

"Brogan has his uses. Figure what that is, or stay clear. You were a cop. You know how that is." Neville removes his hand, leaves me to stand on my own. "You know, you should have come to me when you fell into trouble with him."

"I did go looging for you." When was that? In another life. What did I want?

"That's right. You left word at the laundry. And Malcolm said you'd been by his place. I came quickly as I could, but you'd already run into Brogan again."

"Who hired the kid'th lawyer?"

"The lawyer for Gretchen? Her family I expect."

I shake that off. "The other one. Jathon. The lawyer that let him confeth to murder. Who'th paying hith bill?"

"I don't know all the details of course, but you don't need to worry. As I understand it, Jason believed Doggo was the cause of Gretchen's problems, leading the girl to sex and drugs. So he put an end to it. If he didn't kill Doggo, suspicion falls on the girl. Either way, Jason confessed and Brogan has let you go."

"Maybe Jathon did Doggo, but he wathn't aroun' Thaturday to do Toby. The confethion won't hold. He came downtown Thunday after Toby hit the newth. Jathon thoughd Gredchen needed hith help."

We both laugh at the idea of Gretchen needing help. It hurts. "Point ith, I want to be thure I don't hire Jathon's lawyer."

"You don't need a lawyer, John. If you do, I'll see you get a good one." He sees how I walk. "You've been cornholed. It's hard not to take that personally, but you must try. It's just what they do, police procedure." For Brogan, at least. "They fingered a British lawyer here on vacation last year. Dragged him off the street as he passed the station. Strip search. Cavity search."

"Why don't they ever thay that in the touritht brothures?"

Neville nods. "That's the spirit. Actually, it turned into something like that. When the mayor got wind, after the Brit went home and complained, he invited the poor sod back, on the taxpayer's arm of course, to make amends."

"He came bag?"

"Of course not. I can't help wondering what the mayor had in mind for second prize, though, can you?"

"You're telling me nod to come bag to Toronto?"

"Nothing so drastic." He catches my arm again. "But let it go. Or else it eats you up inside. Understand?"

I push on. "Could you?"

"Had to," he says. "It's hard. Hanging on to a grudge is worse."

Neville leads me slowly into the Java Hut at the corner. Concrete steadies under my heels. "Let's get you cleaned up."

He greets the man behind the counter as we walk through to a rear door. "Morning Danny. Have a couple ready when we get back eh, large? Double cream for me. Mr. Swan prefers tea, I think."

"Milk and sugar?" the counterman asks.

"Clear, isn't it John?"

Downstairs is a large, clean, red-and-white tiled washroom.

Neville stuffs paper towels into the drain, runs cold water for me. "I'll wait upstairs, have Danny bag some ice for you. Come up when you're done. We'll talk."

I'm alone with my reflection in the mirror. Not too bad, maybe. Swelling, bruising, but all the big pieces still connected. I blame the door I ran into for most of the damage: two coon eyes with a road-bump between. I stick my face in the sink, come up and start with a paper towel. Some of the scratches aren't scratches at all, just blood-crusted wrinkles. I work around the nose, try to blow it clear. That hurts. I get it straightened out, stuff some paper towel in to give it shape, keep it from re-plugging with blood. Fresh water in the sink, stick my head under again, wash out my hair, dampen a towel and daub at my clothes. Some of the dirt moves, but the bloodstains swell.

If it had been Rajiit waiting outside the cop-shop like a friend with a get-out-of-jail card, there'd also have been a car. Not a big one. A little grey, Japanese hatchback. He would sooner sponsor his kids' soccer team than buy a new car. Still, with Rajiit I'd have had a place to go, and a way to get there.

"Spend the night with us," he'd have said. "Melba insists."

Then he'd have made me go back. "I have assured Detective Brogan I will present you when he next needs you."

Neville may be questionable as a friend. He preaches something like forgive-and-forget. But so far he hasn't said anything about going back to Brogan again. I can almost smell the burning motor oil as I drive Rajiit out of my mind.

Check the mirror again. There I am, nearly as fresh as the rubbies who sleep next door in the streetcar turn-round.

Hot tea and an ice pack waiting when I get back upstairs.

Neville looks me over. "I've seen worse," he says.

"I've come home worth from a drunk," I admit. "But only the oneth."

The tea's hot. One sip makes me cringe. The old fillings, and a new chip for sure.

"Need a doctor?" he asks. "Get that nose looked at?"

"Mnuh. I thuppothe I thould thank you."

He shakes his head. "This is what friends do, John."

"But, you're a buthy man. You could have thent thomeone."

"As in 'you scratch my ass, I'll send someone to scratch yours?' That's not what friends do."

I don't much like the image of Neville scratching my ass. "I'm thtraight, Neville."

"Of course you are. You've been following that Meg woman around all weekend like a confused puppy." He reaches across and pats the back of my hand. "Your manhood's safe with me."

So I'm in Neville's debt, but it's not my fifty-year-old, three-hundred-pound body he's after.

"Cartwright send you to spring me from Brogan?"

He tries to look surprised. "Why would he do that?"

"You tell me. I thaw you with him Thaturday."

"That's how rumours get started," he says, trying to laugh me past the association with Cartwright. "Take last night at Olde Woodbine. When the cruisers came in, sirens wailing, people came out in their robes and pajamas. A rumour started that a motorcycle gang armed with AK-47s had killed all the construction workers and taken over the unfinished houses for a clubhouse. Someone else said a gang of squeegee kids had squatted and taken an innocent real-estate agent hostage. The mayor was supposed to offer himself as a substitute so decent people would feel safe buying houses in Toronto. It's silly of course."

"Uh-huh, but there's thomething in that motorcycle thtory," the jaw and tongue loosening with heat and exercise. "Wann't it you men-tioned Johnny Pops the other day? Pops was killed to make room for the bikers in Ontario."

It's still dark out, but Java Hut's business has started to quicken. Day labourers and insomniacs after that first hit of caffeine. "Thith one of your partnerthips?"

"I own this franchise. And a couple more in Scarborough."

Shit. This was where Meg and I shook down Doggo the Squeegee Boy. This was where we talked strategy. Have shifts of countermen with big ears kept Neville up to date with our plans?

"I saw you with Cartwright Saturday, having a cozy meal over in The Beaches."

"We're both businessmen, John. What's unusual about a business luncheon?"

"Nothing, but naturally I athk myself what busineth you two would have in common. And I also have to ask myself why it is you show up and thpring me just as Cartwright's lawyers tholve Toby and Doggo's murders."

"Do the two have to be connected, John?"

"Of courth they're fucking connected. I've been down here at The Farm maybe a dozen weekends and you've thpoken more to me in the last five minutes than in the last five years." I stand, steady myself. "I'll tell you what I know, becauth I'm already on retainer. The old money behind Cartwright, O'Keefe, bought me off, or didn't Cartwright tell you that?

"You're running a line and loan sharking, with cash flow that needth cleaning up. Cartwrightth got real estate projecth need investment. Gee, I answered my own question. Your busineth connection ith money laundering. But now, thince you two are partnerth, you can't let thith meth hith thtepdaughter made interfere with buthiness. So he lawyerth up the kid, Jason, and you come get me out of jail, find out what I told Brogan. Oh look: I've answered my thecond quethtion."

Out the door leaving the ice pack and cold tea on the table beside Neville's empty cup. Neville catches up before I get next door at the streetcar turn-round. A rubby testing sleep on a bench in the grit-dim folds his collar over his eyes as we pass, making us go away.

"I don't think you've quite got the whole picture, John. For starters, nobody sends me anyplace I don't want to go."

I walk again, faster. Or maybe I only think it's faster because I'm breathing harder. I pull the paper out of my nose. Bleeding's stopped, for now. I'm still not leaving Neville in my dust.

"Okay, we'll do it your way. What did you tell Brogan?"

"We're quit the shit now, are we? I didn't say anything to Brogan about anything except me falling into that basement and finding Squeegee Boy stuffed behind the furnace." I'm slurring less now.

"It's good to know you can be trusted to keep a confidence. The point is to keep our associations quiet while this Gretchen mess is fixed."

"Yeah, well, don't get cocky. Brogan found the cheque O'Keefe gave me." Shit. I dig into my pockets, my wallet. The cheque's gone. "He kept it."

One bulb in an apartment foyer we pass on the street. Not bright enough to help me find anything in the dark recesses of my wallet.

Neville pulls his dark hand from a deep pocket. O'Keefe's cheque is between his fingers. "Brogan's not a problem," he says. "You're right about Cartwright. He doesn't have any money of his own. But if he were backed entirely by the father-in-law, he wouldn't need me now would he?" He hands me the paper, wraps an arm around and shoulders me further down the street. "Don't think ill of the old man. He meant well, and his situation is only temporary, but he's overextended at the moment and can't quite get used to the idea of not having cash on hand. The cheque's worthless I'm afraid. Shame, really, just as the son-in-law is so eager to expand."

Off the apartment building's right shoulder is the dark square box of the Italian's café. It would be nice, now, to have the shadow of the thick Italian glowering out the front window, witness to Neville guiding me down the street.

"Overextended because he's got the sudden expense of defending a custody suit while his money's tied up in Olde Woodbine Estates?"

Neville's gone quiet on me. "A custody battle…did that give you access to their financial records? You used Toby and the custody suits, to get to Cartwright. Is that how you found out Cartwright had the kid, Gretchen, muling drugs to the 'burbs for him?"

"You're a good detective, John. I knew that, soon enough, you'd have it all figured out on your own."

An empty lot, mostly paved, filling with weeds. A row of narrow Victorian brick houses, windows still dark.

"Not to be immodest, John, but I'm known for helping people with their problems around here. Can you appreciate that? I often

make people's troubles go away. Toby saw Gretchen in this neighbourhood, on her own, weekends. He became concerned. He
brought his concerns to me. That's perfectly natural. I don't like to
speak ill, but Toby had his own problems coping. I've had to help him
with personal difficulties in the past. Still, it was clear that Gretchen
required more supervision than her mother and stepfather were
providing. So we found a lawyer with expertise in such things. In the
end we found a solution to everybody's benefit. So you see, I'm something of a street counsellor."

"Understand you were a doctor, back in the Caribbean?"

"A bit of an overstatement I'm afraid. I was a veterinarian. That's
how I first came to this corner of the city, working the stables at the
track before it was torn down. Still, a conscientious man in that position hears things and learns to help out where he can."

Dim light from the interior of the liquor store. No cabs waiting
to pick up fares making home deliveries.

"What help was Toby supposed to get?"

"Custody of Gretchen, naturally."

"Lucky him," I say. "You might have killed Toby to put him out
of his misery."

"I wouldn't hurt Toby. It's not my way."

"I've heard about your medical specialty." I drag my feet, but this
morning I'm in no shape to resist. Neville shoulders me along.

"Really? You have been busy. But surely the benefit of the ideal
threat is never having to implement the consequence. Not more than
once, at least. And why should I harm Toby if he is so useful to me?"

"Say he flaps his gums. Once you and Cartwright are linked up,
Toby gets expendable in a hurry."

Neville won't have it. "That is the thing about you police, you
really must get this idea out of your mind, always dealing in "take-
away." Someone doesn't behave, they break some tiny, obscure law
and you would take away their freedom, or take away some of their
money at the very least. And so often it is taken away from those who
can ill afford it. Then you wonder why you are not held in higher
esteem."

We're stopped outside the hotel. No light on in the room front
right. I want to go in. I don't want to go in. If Meg's up there, I'm not
going to bring Neville to her.

"The world so full of opportunity and we have this system to stop people realizing their potential. They call that justice? I always kept a place for Toby in my enterprise, even though he could be a bit, shall we say, unusual, odourous? Nobody ever credited what Toby said, even if he'd understood half of it himself. There's opportunity for you too, John, if you could only see it."

He loosens his grip, steps around to face me, a hand loosely on each of my shoulders. I bolt, hobble around the side into the hotel parking lot. Two cars in the building's shadow, rocking on their springs, the pavement that absorbed Toby's blood littered with used rubbers and hypos. Brogan was right about the hotel. I should never have brought Meg here. If I can get to the rear drive, out to the side street and maybe lost in the residential backyards, lead Neville away from the hotel and Meg.

Around the corner, coming my way: Cecil.

XXIV

He flicks the same steel he showed me Friday night at The Farm. "Well, here we all together again. You two chatting so nice and pretty soon old Cecil's name bound to come up."

"That you Cecil?" Neville says behind me. "I've been so worried, looking for you." Something in Neville's voice, something I could mistake for sincerity if I didn't know better. I stumble on the rough pavement, get my balance. Caught between ex-lovers. Feeling like a fool.

"Sure. You don't need to worry yourself. Cecil looking after Cecil now. You not taking care of business for sure."

"I've seen Cecil," I call back. "Since Friday." Saturday at The Farm, chatting with Sweetie Mack, the two breaking away when they saw me watching. And I remember thinking how strange to see Cecil without Neville.

Cecil pushes me back into his ex-boss. "Go on, tell him. Cecil want to see his face while he find out."

"He's cut a deal," I say. "Haven't you Cecil? With Sweetie Mack."

"I here just waiting for you to go inside, take Neville on his own walk. You should have gone inside, Mr. Swan."

Neville is behind me still, but his voice is strange, tight. "Not now Cecil. Business is better than ever. I've even got us a penthouse in the Towers of Olde Woodbine."

"Better for Neville, you mean. What do Cecil get?"

"What do you want? Clothes, cards. All you have to do is ask."

"Sure, Cecil be your butler maybe, fetch your pipe and slippers in your new apartment? Then you tired, throw Cecil out. That's okay.

Cecil likes the street. The street is who Cecil is. People see me, they know Cecil comin.'"

A sliver of light, the side door from the hotel opening behind Cecil, closing again.

"You want the gambling, the laundry? It's yours. Anything. Whatever you want, just don't leave me Cecil."

"Forget it Neville," I interrupt. "He's already committed, aren't you Cecil? You told Toby the change in command and he refused to turn on Neville, the man who gave him a job and was helping to get his kid back. Or did Toby see you Saturday with Sweetie, like I did, and make his own conclusions?'"

Cecil's head shaking, "I knew he would tell Neville if I give him the chance."

Behind me I sense Neville's coat opening, a weapon slipping into his hand. Cecil not considering his former lover might be armed, not knowing his boss could do murder because that was what Neville had always kept him for.

"So you didn't even give him a chance. You lured him to this lot on Saturday night, made sure he stayed quiet."

"There you go, smart man," he says, moving to close the gap between us, his blade arcing.

I raise my arms to block, anticipate the searing edge across my palm, bone-scrape, white pain. A long, low, scream begins as I will Neville to shoot the son of a bitch. *Shoot him, don't you see you'll be next?* Nothing.

I drop my arms, Cecil's smile fades, sweat shining black in reflected light, his eyes rolling, a bubble of sour breath pops from his mouth as he sinks, and Meg's face rises behind, her curls falling back to rest.

It pours out in a gush. "He's been watching the hotel all day, since I came and re-registered. From across the road at first," she says. "When Stan came I took him with me and pretended to run into Cecil. All Cecil talked about was you, where he could find you. Then you came to the theatre and I had to get rid of you without Cecil following."

My knees wobble. The screaming has stopped. Might have been me. Cars throw gravel escaping the lot. A window closes upstairs in the hotel. My tongue doesn't work. I point to what Meg holds in her hand.

"I put it in my purse back home, remember, when I went back in for my toothbrush." She raises the sack of weighted leather, my sap, a piece of Cecil's scalp still clinging to the seam. "Did I do it right?"

"Shit yes," I spit out. "Hit him again if you want," putting my shoe in Cecil's ear.

"Stop. Please." It's Neville, sliding down the brick hotel wall, the heel of one hand in his eye, the other raised palm out to Meg and I. There's no gun. Maybe there never was.

"He planned to kill us, Neville. He had to. He'd gone over to Sweetie and was terrified you'd found out, thought we were plotting against him."

"I don't care. Enough. Don't hurt him any more." Neville's other hand, I realize now, holds a cellphone. Both his cheeks glisten. "I'll look after it. Someone to come, clean this up. Just don't hurt him anymore."

His eyes are full. "Go. I don't want to see either of you again. Ever."

XXV

I gather Meg. "After the movie Cecil and Stan walked me back to the hotel. I wouldn't let them come up, but they didn't leave. I saw them from the room window, talking on the sidewalk." Guiding her around to the front door. "Cecil went into the parking lot. So I stayed at the window in case you came back. I was going to warn you, but you went around the side by the time I came downstairs. So I came around the back."

"What about Stan? Where'd he go?"

"Across the street, drinking coffee all night in the window of Henry's Beautiful Hamburgers, keeping an eye, making sure Cecil didn't come up I guess."

I'm already gone. Stan Walters has left his perch in Henry's, ambling toward the restaurant's door. He may have been an athlete once, but his knees are shot. Good thing because I'm a bit slow myself, being old and fat and having had a copper's baton up my ass all night. I come up on him as he opens the door on a big, black 4-by-4 nosed into a parking slot. I slam the door before he can get inside, jamming him up against the truck body.

"You're all right then," he says. "Cecil had me worried there for minute."

"Fuck you were. You were spotting for him, signal when I went inside." A couple slaps across the top of his head, delivered over the window.

"I could take you in a fair fight," he says.

"That's why we won't have one." Pull him out by his thin hair,

186

drag him to the front of the truck, shielded from the street and restaurant windows. "You think this is the schoolyard, Stan?" Spin him. A right to his gut. "Fucking fair fight my ass."

He spits and wheezes like a dying spray can. "Saw...saw...you...that man. H...have you arrested."

Pull him up by the hair. "Shut the fuck up." Punch my fist into his throat.

Stan's hands grasp at his neck. I let go. He's working too hard sucking air to hit or run.

"Here's how I see it..."

He still can't find wind, shakes his head between wheezes.

"You could have gone after her anytime since Ham's death. But you didn't until she started hanging around with me, an ex-cop. Make that an ex-detective. You were afraid she'd start talking about you and Ham down at the cottage dock." Shit, I'd practically told him she had, yesterday afternoon in the theatre lobby.

He coughs and spits, head and hands shaking: "Meg. Meg was there too."

"Yeah, only she wasn't getting hit on by Ham. You were, and that's why you drowned him."

"No," he coughs again. "No, I mean Meg was there when...when Ham died."

"When you killed him." He ducks, expecting me to hit him again. "Go ahead, say it Stan. Confession's good for the soul." Help it along with another slap.

He nods. "It was an accident. I pushed him away. He fell. In shallow water. Must have hit his head. I could have got him out, but I just stood there, with Meg, watching." Stan starts to cry.

"There, easy eh? Now your penance so you'll feel all better. Give me your wallet."

His eyes bulge. "Don't you understand? Meg was there. She's as guilty as I am."

"Fuck Stan, high-school coach like you, you should know life's a team sport. Right now, you're on the losing team. Give me your wallet."

He fumbles in his jacket. I grab his wrist, pull his hand out, reach in, take out the billfold myself, flip through his ID.

"I'm telling you the truth. Meg was there too."

"Truth's for saps and poets, Stan. I don't give a shit." Here's what I'm looking for, pull out the ownership to his truck. "There, sign the pink."

"It's not pink."

"No, it's pink in California where they make all the car movies. Jesus shit, why am I wasting time telling you this? Sign the fucking thing." I slap him again.

"I don't have a pen!"

"Christ, what kind of teacher doesn't carry a pen? Now I got to tie you up, stuff you somewhere until..."

"There's one in the glove compartment."

I count over two hundred dollars in his wallet, while he pens the pink on the truck hood. He gets his wallet with a crisp twenty for bus fare home when he hands me the ownership.

"Say anything about this, just remember, you're in it as thick as Meg. Gimme the keys." He pulls them out of his pants pocket. "And put that pen back in the glove compartment. Don't want you shorting me on this deal."

I'm running on pure adrenaline, spitting it out as it comes to me, not sure of any of it until this shakedown. Couldn't prove a word of it. Now, him giving up the truck is proof enough.

Fucking thing drives like a dream.